The author is 19 years old and this is her first novel. She wrote *Fallen from Grace* when she was 17.

She has been reading thrillers from a young age and draws inspiration from those. A lot of the themes are adapted from her personal experiences. She has designed the characters from influential people in her life.

Sarah hopes to help people who are going through mental health illnesses.

Dearest Sarah,
Thought you had secretly written your autobiography when I saw this title but it's a thriller (rather badly) written by a (not very literate) 17 year old. W xxx

For Mum, Anna, Luke and Jade.

Sarah Heywood

FALLEN FROM GRACE

AUSTIN MACAULEY PUBLISHERS™

LONDON • CAMBRIDGE • NEW YORK • SHARJAH

A CIP catalogue record for this title is available from the British
Library.

ISBN 9781528927536 (Paperback)
ISBN 9781528965118 (ePub e-book)

www.austinmacauley.com

First Published (2019)
Austin Macauley Publishers Ltd
25 Canada Square
Canary Wharf
London
E14 5LQ

Jessica walked towards the crime scene lost in the feeling of tiredness. This wasn't the first time. She had been to countless crime scenes. Declan was waiting by his car for her. She was quite late to the scene. She glanced down at her wristwatch, twenty minutes past. Twenty minutes late. She stared up at the sky. The clouds had been painted orange by the sunset. She was suddenly blinded by the flash of a camera bulb. *Damn paparazzi.* She shielded her face from the lens of the cameras. There weren't many there but they were always persistent. It was always the same. The vans parked bumper to bumper, each reporter pushing and cheating for the story. They were different but no better than the criminals they wrote about. Some of them.

Jessica felt an invisible blow to the stomach. She slid her left leg back, she was excepting the hit. This was a bad one. She knew instantly it was the vigilante. She could always tell. That's what made her a good detective. She knew things. As though she could see them before they happened. The Fallen Angel was back. She tensed her hands and tightly shut her eyes. She had dealt with them on a case last year. They had found the body in a forest a few miles away. The Angel had killed a man for abducting a young girl. They tracked the note and found the girl locked inside an abandoned building. They were too late to save her but they would never have found her without the Angel.

The first question that came to her was how they found out about these crimes? Jessica brought her hand to her stomach and gripped her shirt. The pain was getting worse. She wiped her brow with the corner of her sleeve.

All the cases had etched away at her. She had seen hidden disease run through the city. Unseen—until it reared its ugly head.

It was a man with frosted lips and pale skin. His face was pulled back into the wrinkle that had been cut deep. *Late fifties,* Jessica thought. She could tell from the discolouration on his skin.

He was wearing the bottom half of a dark business suit and perfectly polished black shoes. It was a high quality brand—a rich man.

"You already know it's the Angel."

He gestured down to the victims back. She nodded and looked down at his bare back. The Angel always left two long slits down their victims' back. Like the mark of wings. Blood was still spilling from his shoulder, the blades pushing up against the exposed flesh.

"I figured it was."

She crouched down next to the body. His face was badly beaten. She leaned forward and noticed a small piece of paper lodged beneath the body. She pulled across his right arm, limply pushing it above his head. She took a second and when she spoke her voice was softer. She used the femininity to assert her power.

"I need an evidence bag. I found the note."

She reached across and carefully pulled the note out.

She unfolded it, as blood dripped onto the cobblestone roadside. She rubbed her thumb across the smooth surface, revealing a note written in neat handwriting. Declan held the open evidence bag beside her. She slipped it into the bag and stood up. Jessica looked past him and watched the techs checking the area for prints.

The note read small details of different crimes, each one committed by the man who lay now like trash at the side of the road. Jessica knew what that meant. It was the calling card of the famed vigilante who had been responsible for so many previous crimes. The media had named them the Fallen Angel, in that the Angel wanted justice but had become like the criminals they despised.

She took off her blue gloves, remembering the code when dealing with the Fallen Angel. The more violent the death, the worse the crimes. It reminded her of something she had once read, but she could never remember what. It annoyed her. It's funny how the mind wanders sometimes.

Stanley Watts, the coroner's assistant, came marching into the tarp. An annoyed groan escaped Jessica's lips. Two large men followed behind him. They nodded at Jessica and lifted the body up onto the black stretcher. Watts zipped up the bag. The body was bloated and filled the plastic.

"The coroner will take a look in the van," said Watts. "Media are everywhere."

"Why?"

"Don't you know who the victim is?"

He unzipped the bag down to the corpse's chest and pointed down, a smug smile spreading across his face. He knew something she wanted and he was going to play with it. Tease her. Jessica looked down at the body and examined the features. His face was so beaten she couldn't tell who it was. An instant sense of nausea hit her.

"No, who is he?"

Jessica was nervous and for a second no one moved.

"Callum Hart. Entrepreneur and third richest man in London."

Jessica squirmed a little when he said it. She crouched down besides the building again, staring at the puddle of blood for a moment before standing up and leaving the cover of the tarp. The coroner's van was parked across the field under the cover of a graffiti-covered building. Declan followed her to the coroner's van and opened the van door. The strong smell of flesh hit her as she stepped in. The coroner stood over the body, the bag unzipped. He wore a blue jumpsuit, covering his expensive suit. He had a cleanly shaven head and thick muscular arms. Sweat dripped down his tanned forehead and onto his thick eyebrows. Suddenly, he seemed depressed. He turned away from the body. Watt gripped his shoulder and squeezed it tightly. He pulled away and stepped back into the light above the body. He looked tired; his shoulders were slumped down. He had done this job for years and it was starting to take it out of him.

Once he noticed the detectives, he stood up and unzipped the jumpsuit down to his waist. He wore a purple-striped tie tight around his thin neck. His red dragon tattoo peeked out from his collar. The van was ice-cold as the wind bashed against the metal side, echoing through the tight space. He spoke in a heavy accent and used British to assert his authority. But he was still good at it, and still had the passion in his eyes when he stood before a body, this made him a legend in the department and someone Jessica had the deepest respect for.

"Detective Denning."

"What have you got for me?"

He rolled off his gloves and threw them down on the shelf behind. He flicked the lid of a bottle of Evian and gulped it down. The water trickled down his neck and onto his crisp white collar. He was expected to be very masculine but he showed quite the opposite as he looked at the body and tears filled his eyes.

"It was definitely the vigilante who killed him, you can tell from the severity of his wounds. No defensive wounds, but he was restrained by the wrists, and the cause of death was a single bullet in the head."

He knelt back down, zipped up the black bag, and covered the body. His knees were covered in lime grass stains. He scrubbed hard at them and grunted.

Jessica felt her chest tighten as the smell of decaying flesh filled the small space. She pushed out of the door, breathing in the clean air in a large gulp, sickness fading from her stomach. Declan leaned against the side of the van and fired up his e-cig. Apocolypse bubbleum. Jessica loved the bright blue colour of the liquid. He pressed the button five times in quick succession, the pen it up and beeped. He breathed in the smoke in long heavy drags. He blew clouds of smoke towards Jessica. The strawberry scent cleared her lungs. He jumped back up to his feet and slipped his e-cig back into his jacket pocket.

"What's the plan?"

"I want to go back to the station and review the evidence."

She signalled over to the crowds of reporters.

"We'll need to get through there."

"I'll sort it."

Declan made his way through the crowds of reporters, stood behind the yellow tape. Jessica waited behind, glaring at her watch. She was hungry, but she knew she wouldn't have time to eat.

When Declan cleared the path, he signalled Jessica over.

As Jessica pushed through the group of people, a young reporter stood straight in front of her and blocked her path. She was wearing a short skirt suit. A cameraman stood directly behind her and pointed the lens close to Jessica's face. Jessica felt her temperature rise as the woman walked closer holding a microphone.

"Detective. What exactly has happened here?"

Jessica pushed forward. The crowd of reporters gathered to try and catch the interview. They began to swarm around her like flies. If only she could swat them away.

"No comment."

"Is it true that the victim is famous entrepreneur, Callum Hart?"

Jessica knew it was Watts who leaked things to the press. He thought the camera loved him but he loved the attention.

"I'm not at liberty to discuss any details of the case at this time."

Jessica began to walk away. But the woman followed close behind her, making sure the camera stayed focused on them both.

"Do you have any leads on the allusive vigilante?"

"No comment."

"What did Callum Hart do to end up victim to the Fallen Angel?"

Jessica turned around and came within an inch of the woman's face. And began to scrutinise her features. There was nothing recognisable about her. She didn't look like what Jessica would have imagined. Her white hair looked off against her Caucasian skin. Jessica curled her lips into a knowing smile.

"I cannot confirm or deny anything at this time. My team and I will review and follow the evidence until it yields a result. Thank you."

Jessica walked around to the driver's side of her car and slid into the leather seat. The cameraman followed as the car sped off. He kept it running until the tail lights had disappeared.

Jessica drummed her hands on the wheel. She tried to make a tune. But it was off and frantic. It nearly made her smile. Nearly. Declan turned and leaned towards Jessica. He picked up the evidence bag from the space between the seats.

He studied it. The ink was thick and heavily laid on. He rubbed across it with one of his huge hands. After staring at it, he concluded the writer had used their dominant hand, and from the direction of each letter's curves, it was their right. He shook his head. That didn't tell them anything.

"Angela Moss
Delia Moran
Jackie Curtis
Rhonda Hampton
His life for the four
He stole."

He folded the note over in the evidence bag before shoving it into his case, the four names burning in his head. He looked back across at Jessica. He would have smiled but he knew the case was too serious. He was bothered by something but was not quite sure what. His thoughts were mixed. Swirling in his head. He wasn't meant to care. But in that moment he was glad the bastard was dead.

Callum Hart was a very rich and influential man. What had made his name and face so well known in London was his work in the media.

To the outside world he kept his image up. Supporting minority groups and offering money like it was nothing. But behind closed doors he was abusive. His countless women would often end up in hospital.

His last wife, Rhonda Hampton was well known for owning a chain of high-end hotels. Hampton hotels, London. She was always at some event or another, heavily plastered over the news. But once she married Callum her social life changed and she rarely left the house.

The last injury her private hospital had recorded was a broken rib cage, just weeks before she disappeared.

Most people assumed she had just had enough and left him. Wishful thinking.

Jessica now knew differently because her body was laying in the morgue. Along with the bodies of his three previous wives.

They had been hidden beneath the ground for so long most of the flesh had been torn from their bodies. The neck was still carefully preserved in plastic wrap. She studied it for a moment.

"Detective Denning," the pathologist said. Interrupting her thoughts. He was wearing a grey pinstripe suit and a black tie. The deep lines on his face curled into a smile. Whenever he looked at Jessica she knew he was the only man she would ever love.

"What have you got for me?"

Her neck was stiff and in pain from standing so long. She pulled at the skin, brushing along the raised hairs. She noticed an empty chair and sat down. The pathologist nodded and spoke,

"Most of the body has decayed over time and can't tell us much. But the neck has been preserved."

That bothered her for some reason. Why commit this ritual after death. She shook her head and managed a smile. Wiping the thought from her mind.

"Luckily for you, the neck tells us the cause of death and who did it."

Jessica felt her pulse lift a bit. She swallowed deep and hard. The pathologist cleared his throat.

"I can tell you that once again the Angel got it right. Callum Hart was responsible for these deaths."

Jessica focused her eyes on him. The words crossed the room but sounded so out of place. It was never this easy.

"How can you tell?"

She asked raising one of her eyebrows towards him.

"Callum Hart was known for wearing a personalised wedding band. And it left a very distinct cut on each victim's neck."

He looked down at Hampton's neck. Jessica followed the direction of his eyes and saw the mark. The scar lightly spelled out

'HART' in all caps. Then it made sense why he had carefully preserved the neck. It was a trophy. Like an artist signing his work. She felt her mouth go dry. The though ran down her spine. He possessed them even after he killed them. The pathologist grabbed his coffee and slipped his finger through the handle for balance.

"Do you mind? Some people are touchy around the dead."

Jessica shook her head and smiled. She wasn't touchy anymore. It was just another day at work now. He took a sip and put the mug back down. The sound as it hit against the metal shot through the stale atmosphere.

She thought about it and realised, however, she was witnessing this horror and it just meant one thing; they hadn't done their job. They hadn't checked after any of the women who disappeared. That was on them. She wanted to go back and change it. Save at least one. She had learnt to cope most days. But today was a dark, bleak day.

She remembered the times she imagined using her service pistol. She had planned the whole thing making sure she was alone. Walking into the place where she lived with her brother and going into the top bedroom. The carpets would be hard to clean but she wanted people to notice. It always annoyed her how quickly people forgot. She wanted it to plant in there head like the bullet. She would sit on the bed with the pistol to her head and all the pain would end. But Jessica would never do it. She couldn't add any more suffering. The job had become all she was. But thinking about a release sounded so sweet. She could almost taste the metal tang of blood in her mouth.

Her eyes were on the floor. It didn't sit right. She stood up from the chair and turned to leave.

"Detective, I know I shouldn't say anything but the justice system can't catch everyone and that's not going to change. The Angel catches the ones that slip through the net."

"What do you mean?"

He focused his eyes on Jessica's. They had an almost twisted happiness burning behind them.

"The world is not just split into right or wrong. The Angel walks on the line between the two."

There was something poetic about his words. Jessica hesitated. It was a statement that touched on her private thoughts about the case. And then suddenly it clicked and made sense in her head. No one had caught the angel because no one wanted to. She was doing the world a favour. That thought almost silenced the guilt. She wanted to say something but no words came to her mind.

"Where are you?"

Jessica looked at the tall steel gates and pushed on the carved handle. She wanted to tell him about her past and release her demons and how she failed to protect her brother. How she was scared, that she heard his voice inside her head. She stopped herself.

"At home. I'll be in soon."

She hung up and headed in. The anger and frustration were still seething in her head. The stone sign in front read Dissington Hall. The street that looped around the park was well lit. The grass was neatly cut and dark green. The murmur of sprinkles was the only noise she could hear.

She knew Luke would have never wanted to be here. The city had put him here but no one visited.

She hated visiting her brother's grave. It always filled her with a deep sadness. The grave sat at the end of a long row. She walked down the stone path and stopped in front of the tombstone. She felt a slight pull in her throat as she made to walk. The sound of her steps against the gavel was almost imperceptible against the quiet and for a moment she didn't move. She had been pushing it down for so long there was almost nothing left.

The stone was old and worn. It made her realise how long it had been since her brother had died. That thought sent shivers everywhere. She could feel umps push through her skin. She bent down and picked up the bunch of wilting flowers that lay limply on the ground. It reminded her of the victims arm. Green moss had been growing in between the letters.

'Here lies Luke Denning

A son and brother.

His spirit is everywhere, even in the trees

The words were so plain and unfeeling—the cities choice. Their idea of a heartfelt message. In truth, she could have stopped it but she didn't. She didn't stop any of it. The thought was too much so she focused back on the words.

What did they even mean? Nothing. Pointless and empty words. She shook her head. They made no sense. He had been much more than that to her.

She once again thought about her father. He didn't even know where his son was buried and he didn't care. There was no sadness anymore—there was rage.

She knelt at the foot of the grave and remembered the times she'd find her brother crying and alone. *You are my sunshine* rang in her head. She thought of how her brother had sang it to her every night to cover the screams from the orphanage. She hitched the tears back in her throat. Her eyes were red and wet. She looked like she always did after she drank. She stopped drinking but still always looked broken.

She picked up the photograph that was stuck in the loose ground. She lifted it slowly afraid it would tear apart. The colours had wept and faded. They looked silly but happy. She was dressed as a pumpkin and he was a skeleton. The only picture that anyone ever bothered to take of them. Her eyes watered. She blinked away the tears and opened her eyes. She stared at it as though it were a TV screen. The picture had been taken in the late nineties. The edges under the plastic were still bright with colour. She looked around, at each grave, looking for support.

They were stood in front of a pebble-dashed house, where they had lived as kids. One of many. She looked closer at the image and saw his small birthmarks on his neck. Hidden behind the lobe on his left ear. It was shaped like a butterfly. With small circles at the bottom of the wings.

She rubbed her tattoo and looked closer at the picture. She smirked at his perfect bowl haircut and her long fringe. She flashed back to when she was ten.

She sat on his gaming chair and breathed in the smell of Lynx deodorant. Luke walked over and rested his hand on her back. There carer was lying in bed Too much booze. Their carer often left for two or three days. Every time Luke's shoulders deflated along with his relief. She missed her brother so much. His voice was soft and reassuring—she believed him. Whatever he said. She always blindly followed. Like a dog to its master. She heard that voice now while she sat closer to the grave. She couldn't help but wish there was someone there to comfort her, but there was never anyone. She closed her eyes and tried to conjure back the memory. The rage was good; it distracted her from the pain. It was simple and yet that dark.

She looked at her watch. It was ten thirty. She lay the new bunch of flowers down and ran out of the graveyard, throwing up in the nearest bush.

Back in the car, she was just crying thinking of her brother's smile. Pain flooded into her chest. She was desperate for a drink. Something strong. Whiskey was her favourite. Simple, strong taste and quick. She tried to fight through the pain—but it was an unbearable pain—a pain that clawed at her insides. She played the radio and hummed along. It took her mind away for a moment. Not like a drink would, but it was something. She leaned her head back. She pulled up outside her flat. The air was getting cool. She didn't want to go in but she heard her brother's voice telling her not to worry. She could have cried right there.

The next morning, Jessica sat at her dining room table and drank her coffee. She had changed without showering so she could go straight to her caffeine fix. The sun melted away the ice on the windows.in the time it took to boil the kettle. Clouding the glass. The dew dripped onto the ledge. Her face lost some of its colour. She let the cigarette burn in her hands and bits of ash dropped onto the table. Her small backyard was made of cracked asphalt. She moved into this apartment about a month ago. It was far from perfect. She sat in silence again for a moment. It was nearly six in the morning. After another silent minute, her phone buzzed against the table. The screen flashed the user ID and she saw it was Declan. She put the phone to her ear. She felt a cold breeze against her neck. Her head was spinning.

"What's up?"

She asked him.

"Jess!"

She could hear the perkiness in his voice; he had an undying optimism that Jessica always envied.

"I've got the tech results you asked for."

There was a long moment of silence, and then she finally spoke.

"I'll be about an hour."

Declan was expecting a different reaction. She hung up and put her cup down in the sink. She was headed to the door when a letter fell onto the mat. Her address was neatly typed on the front. The gold ink seemed to glow. She flipped the envelope over. It was stamped with the police crest. She rubbed a shaking hand across her mouth. This case was one surprise after another. She tore open the seal and pulled out the thin letter. It read:

Detective Jessica Denning,

We have recently seen the local press coverage of your interview with the channel 4 news woman outside the crime scene. As you are taking lead on the Callum Hart case, it is your duty to keep as many details as you can from the press.
Deputy Chief Constable,
Harry Clapton

His secretary had spelt his name wrong.
Jessica laughed under her breath. It lightened the otherwise dire situation. Something about the letter angered her. But she could let it go. She reached in her pocket and pulled out an empty cigarette box.

"Fuck!"

She slammed the box and the letter back on the floor.it hit her she had a habit. A nicotine crutch. But she wouldn't admit it. Her hand was gripped so tight on the door handle that her knuckles turned white.
She blinked as she stepped out of the darkness of the hall and onto the lawn in front of her flat. She tilted her face up towards the sun. She let her skin burn in the rays—it felt damn good.

Arriving at work calmed Jessica. She had worked very hard to get to be on the homicide division. It was one thing she knew her brother would be proud of. It was the one thing that demanded all she had. The dead were always the ones who needed her. Her car smelt faintly sour. It smelt like rain to her. She left the windows open during a rainstorm. She opened the glove compartment and found her police radio and freshening gum. She pushed the tape of 'you are my sunshine' to the side. Not wanting to bring up any more memories. There was nothing else. She took out two pieces of gum and headed out to the station. Jessica moved towards the stairs and started up them.

There were no other cars outside the station. A group of homeless men were sitting next to the statue of the Queen. They all turned towards her. One man-wolf whistled as she walked past. She moved an inch closer, she couldn't help it. She felt she needed to be closer to him. She stopped and studied the man before winking. His mouth fell open. She crossed the small entrance. The bells from the church rang in the hour.

"My God…"

Jessica said nothing. She didn't have to. Jessica realised she was more twisted than anyone knew. She liked the feeling of lining people up and watching them dance. She shook her head, almost as if brushing off the thought. She went into the station. She chose to walk straight to her office. She had already decided not to acknowledge the others, so she nodded telling them to leave her. She had a reputation of a bitch.

The lift door opened. A couple staggered in and stood beneath the mirror. She moved into the lift behind them.

Jessica punched in the code, entered the room and sat across from Declan. She stared at him for a long moment. He always had unbrushed hair and a messy tie. His slim trousers clung to his muscular legs. He drummed his fingers against the hardwood of Jessica's desk and shifted in his seat. He looked down, realising he had torn a line in his trousers. Declan moved away, looked at Jessica. They both nodded.

He stood up and put the report on the desk so they could both see it. He rested his fists on the sides and hitched his shoulders up to his neck. Declan does most of the talking Jessica walks to the window and looked out on Scotland place, crossing her arms and cupping her elbows.

"The tech people have said that the only plausible way the Fallen Angel could have known about the criminals they murder is if they have access to the police radio channel," he said. He had tried to keep his voice steady – but he was worried about the outcome. Jessica turned to look at him, as thought she could tell what he was thinking.

"So they have tapped into our network."

"But we can use this to our advantage."

Jessica pulled down the list of crimes the Angel was believed to be responsible for. The magnet fell onto the tiled floor. Declan bent down and clipped it back onto the board. She studied them in detail before she finished the train of thought.

"They only ever kill people who have damaged or destroyed life," she said finally. She rubbed her forefinger into the comer of her eye rubbing away the crust from sleep. She sat in the plush chair behind her desk.

"If we find any active crimes of this nature, we may be able to catch the Angel."

"I'll find out for you."

Declan lifted the phone. Resting it between the padding of his jacket and his ear. He dialled a long telephone number. He said a short code into the line and waited to hear a click. He passed it across. Declan smiled at Jessica. Jessica tried to smile back. She felt her face burn.

She hung up, grabbing her jacket, which hung limply on the back of her chair. She pushed the phone back and reached in her pocket for a smoke she didn't have. She followed Declan into an elevator at the end of the station. He pushed hard on the elevator button, sending them down to the ground floor. The dull music rang through the tight space. Declan kept his eyes shut—he hated small spaces. The elevator lurched to a stop and the metal door swung open. He stopped and breathed slowly for a moment to collect himself.

Jessica found a parking space opposite a restaurant. It was still open but there weren't many people left—it was late.

They walked five shops down to the alley next to a Starbucks. The building next to it was abandoned and looked like an empty shell. Almost haunted. Jessica instinctively drew her hand up to her belt. It was something she always did. Letting people know she was armed. For safety in a way. She felt the brisk night air against her skin.

They turned the corner and saw a body lying against an industrial bin. The green recycling one. Reuse was sprayed on the side below the city crest. It seemed to mean something against the body. His shirt was open, showing a gun strapped on his belt. Blood had flowed from his neck and onto his chest ruining his clothes. He had a long slid across his neck. His chest tattoo was unmistakable he was a gang member but the way it had been burned told Jessica he was shunned. Jessica pulled her eyes away and looked at the abandoned building. The door was propped open and the room was empty. She noticed the rug at the bottom of the stairs had been folded over. Jessica crossed the hall to the rug. It was stained with blood. She stopped and turned back up the stairs. She heard something—or felt it—footsteps. She ran up the crumbling stairs of the building, but her heel caught on the metal tread of the top step. Her hands slammed against the tile floor to break her fall, shock traveling up her arms as her muscles tensed.

She looked up at the doorway, which was swung open, wind whistling through the frame. She could see a shadow against the grey concrete.

She leaped back onto her feet and chased them out onto the rooftop. The night had stolen the light from the sky, with only one dimly lit streetlight—the rest of the roof was covered in a blanket of darkness. The wind whistled loudly through the ventilation fans. Jessica crouched down behind a ventilation duct—the blades spun frantically next to her head.

The Angel appeared in the circle of light. Jessica watched them as they stared off into the dark night. She brought her eyes up. She realised they had been standing there for about ten minutes. The Angel was right there. Jessica came out of hiding. She spoke in a hushed tone, trying not to scare the Angel off, like she were a timid pet.

"Hello!"

She shifted her stance and then eyed the whole figure in front of her. The Angel's slim, muscular figure caused Jessica's heart to race inside her chest.

"Don't shoot. My name is Detective Jessica Denning."

She examined the face and she couldn't help it; she got lost in her eyes. They were a deep blue almost like the ocean. Jessica bought her eyes to them and realised they were smiling. Jessica kept the gun in her hand but off to the side. She felt her stomach tighten and palms begin to sweat. She was out of control and she didn't like it.

"Aren't you scared?"

The voice was female, strong and confident. The lust soared through Jessica's veins.

She cleared her throat. Her voice slightly hoarse and off pitch, it was a moment before she responded.

"No, why should I be?"

She was flirting, trying to take back the control. She just looked at her. Her make-up consisted of black eyeliner, and thick red lipstick. The perfect image of the male fantasy

"Do you have a name?"

She shouted out over the wind and the sirens that rang below,

"Ava."

Jessica's attention was torn from the moment as she heard the wooden door slam against the brace on the concrete wall. Declan's shoes crunched on the loose stone of the rooftop. He looked at Jessica, his eyes wide with concern. He raised his gun, a slight tremor in his hand. Jessica looked at the Angel and then back at Declan. The Angel was already standing on the edge of the building. She stared down the barrel of the gun. She looked back at Jessica her eyes catching the lights of the city as she winked.

And then she disappeared, vanishing into the dark backdrop of the night.

Jessica and Declan ran over to the ledge and leaned over. The Angel had already disappeared.

"What happened, Jess?"

Jessica turned around and caught Declan's eye contact. Her mood dropped and she felt anger towards Declan. She raised her voice, making it known that he had fucked up.

"I was trying to get close enough to catch them."

"Did they say anything?"

Jessica thought hard for a moment. Her heart was still hammering inside her chest.

"No."

It was after three in the afternoon and Jessica decided to get a Coca-Cola from the machine in the back hall. She nodded at Declan through the window—her way of asking if he wanted one. He shook his head, no. She was replaying Ava's name and voice inside her head. While she leaned against the wall and drank the can, she saw an older couple come through the stairwell door. Jessica could almost smell there desperation. It took them ten minutes to walk across the hall.

The station was almost empty. The woman had been crying. She held a damp tissue to her mouth. She leaned limply on her husband. Beneath his glasses, there was warmth that Jessica liked. The patch over his pocket said his name was Nunez. Jessica remembered the thin file she held in her hand. It had the same name printed on the front. He smiled, showing his pink, receding gums. The woman's face was clouded over. Even with the heavy makeup, Jessica could see it clearly.

"Detective Denning?"

Jessica noticed his voice was higher and more urgent.

"I'm Rose Nunez's father."

Jessica was quite for a moment. She knew everything she said from now could save or destroy the couple. She felt a small stone stop in her chest.

In her mind she pictured Rose. Standing in the dark. Alone. His eyes never left Jessica's. It was as though he was reading her soul. Her history. Jessica adjusted her stance ad turned to the left away from his stare.

"Rose Nunez was taken whilst walking home from work on Tuesday the 18th."

She flipped the file closed. A gentle smile swept across her face. Her voice was soft and quite. Tears rolled down the woman's cheek. Jessica knew that pain.

The desperation in his voice was more than just spoken. He fingered a crucifix which hung around his neck on a thick chain. He loved the feel of it in his thick hands. His daughter had worn its twin since she was young.

She took a step towards them and lowered her voice. Kind of like a child.

"Please, come with me."

The man stood helping up the woman whose body had become weak with grief. She almost fell to her knees as she passed the photo of her daughter pinned to the board. Jessica's positive mood dropped as she stepped into the cold room. Her head followed.

Jessica guided them to the break room and shut the door as the couple sat down on the brown leather sofa in the middle of the room. She walked over sitting on the black chair opposite.

Mrs Nunez cleared her throat, wiping her eyes with a torn piece of tissue. As she spoke, her voice strained and cracked,

"Have you found her?"

The woman was desperate—her hands shaking as she tore her tissue to relieve her stress. Her nails had been bitten down to the beds. They were painted with chipped purple varnish. Blood had dried on each one. Jessica gulped lowering her eyes and shaking her head,

"No."

The woman buried her head in her hands. Sobbing loudly as her palms filled with tears. Her husband reached across and stroked along her back. The woman looked up her eyes filled with pain.

"Did you find her crucifix?"

The husband stared at her with hollow eyes.

Jessica looked at him and shook her head. A tear rolled down his cheek.

"I'm afraid there was nothing of your daughter's left on the scene."

"Of course."

Her husband cupped her into his arms, resting his face against hers. A strip of light spread across the tiled floor. Jessica followed it to a gap in the opened door where Declan was standing. The glass of his watch catching the light and shining it directly into Jessica's eyes.

"I have Mr Nunez here asking to see you."

He pushed the door fully open, the light flooding into the dimly lit room. Next to Declan stood a much taller man with a darker skin tone. His eyes were small and stern but his face was soft with friendly features. As he appeared, Mrs Nunez jumped up from her seat rushing over and embracing the man. She buried her face in the warmth of his chest. As she pulled away she left a damp mark on the front of his shirt from her tears. She rubbed her hand across his cheek his hand reaching up and taking hers. She guided him over to the brown sofa, where he sat between the girl's parents—his hand still locked in Mrs Rogers.

Jessica smiled as she picked up a pen. She opened the notebook in her hand, Mr Nunez could see part of her writing.

But she flicked through it quickly, stopping on the last blank page. Resting the tip against the line of her paper.

"I need to ask you what happened the last time you saw Rose."

Mr Nunez rubbed his gold ring with his thumb before he answered.

"The last time I saw my wife was on the Tuesday morning she left for work as usual but this time she didn't come back. I waited, I even went to her work she wasn't there. I was told she left early, I searched but I couldn't find her."

He gulped, a single tear falling down stopping on his unshaven cheek. Jessica passed over the small box of tissues from the table.

"Do you know of anywhere Rose might go?"

"She would never have left without telling me where she was."

Jessica scribbled what the man was saying down on the yellow, lined page. She looked across at the woman and studied her properly. She was very beautiful; she had a small oval face that looked sad and aged. That was just physical; her personality seemed soft and kind. She turned to look across at the husband. His features were harsher and more defined but his eyes were kind and trusting. His hair was a dull blond and had been messily swept to the side.

A loud knock sounded through the room. The room instantly flooded with light as the door swung open and Declan stepped in to the full view. Declan called into the room, his voice was soft,

"Jessica."

She looked up from her writing and rested the page back on the table before she stood to leave. As she reached the door she turned back towards the family.

"I'm going to find your daughter, I promise."

The woman still gripped tightly to the crucifix in her hand.

"Thank you, detective. Just bring her back to me."

She shut the door following Declan back to her desk, sitting down while she sipped the coffee. Declan sat on the edge of the desk opposite, his arms folded across his lap. She let her mind wander back to Ava. She thought of her face. She thought about her body. The hairs on her arms stood up and her body flushed with heat. Declan grinned to himself as he watched her cheek turn a deep pink. Jessica opened her eyes and saw Declan's grin.

"Did you find anyone close to Rose?"

He gave her another smile and said,

"I spoke to the people who worked with Rose at the Mayor's office."

"Did you find anything?"

"Another secretary said that she overheard an argument between Rose and the Mayor. She said that once Rose left she screamed back through the shut door that she wouldn't be going back."

Jessica stood to leave and drank down the rest of her coke.

"Then we best talk to the Mayor."

When her eyes adjusted to the light, she saw a staircase leading up. Jessica hoped that when she got there, there would be time to gather herself. But a woman was already waiting for them at the top of the stairs. Jessica had worked a case in a conference room once before. That seemed like a long time ago but she remembered it. Jessica identified herself and explained she was on a homicide investigation. It was almost scripted; shed said it so many times. The woman was a beautiful blonde with blue eyes. Her hair was still blonde but flecks of grey had started to appear. One hand was on her hip. The other was holding a mobile phone.

Declan kept his eyes on the floor. Jessica came level with the woman as she reached the top step. She smelled the familiar scent of someone trying to hide their guilty pleasure. She breathed in deeper, hunting out her vice. Smoking.

"Detectives Denning and Hughes. I'll need to see some ID."

Jessica pulled open her jacket, showing her badge clipped to the top of her trousers.

Declan passed the woman his badge. There was a slight tremor in his hands. She studied his badge and typed something into the phone. The brightness from the screen shone onto her face and highlighted the deep lines that ran across it. Like carved marble.

"Thank you, if you'd come with me."

She turned around and walked off. Jessica and Declan followed close behind. The woman stopped outside a large wooden door. A small, gold sign hung from pins in the middle. It was engraved with thick looped letters. 'Mayor's Office.' She tried the locked door and then knocked sharply on the glass. She knocked quietly, poking her head through a gap in the door. She called out,

"I have the detectives here to see you, sir."

A harsh, rough voice mumbled back. The woman then pushed the door open. She stood to the side and gestured the detectives in. Declan closed the door and focused his attention on the room. Jessica practically rolled into the chair. She was tired. The weight of the case was heavy. The Mayor stood up from behind the desk in the centre of the room. Wrinkled lines were carved deep into his face; his small dark eyes were stern and sweat was clinging to his pale skin.
His voice was deep when he spoke, "Welcome Detective, what exactly can I do for you?"

He sat back down in his brown leather chair. Jessica and Declan sat in the metal chairs opposite. Declan pulled himself up to be taller and straightened his tie. Jessica opened the file and put a 6x10 photo on the desk. It showed Rose Nunez. She slid the photo across the desk and the Mayor glanced at it without touching it.

"We're investigating the disappearance of Rose Nunez. The woman in this photo."

Jessica stopped and waited to see if he recognised the name. He looked across at Jessica. His eyes were plain and staring. She couldn't read his expression. Then he turned to Declan. A smile stretched across his face. For a second or more his eyes were fixed on Declan's chest. He leaned across and spoke in a soft whisper, "Detective Hughes, may I get you a drink."

Declan wanted to smile but knew it would be taken wrong. The Mayor leaned back and grabbed a glass decanter from the cabinet behind the desk. He came back with a large glass of scotch. Declan shuffled in his seat and rubbed the glass of his watch. Smudging it. Making it unreadable.

"No thank you. We do need to ask about Mrs Nunez."

"Of course."

"What happened on the Tuesday?"

The Mayor sipped his glass. The scent of scotch was already strong on his breath.

"Rose arrived at work, the same as usual. The only thing that was different was she asked to leave early."

Jessica leaned forward and rested her hands on the edge of the chair.

"We have a witness who overheard an argument between you and Rose. Afterwards, she quit her job and walked out and was clearly upset."

She said, the Mayor looked over. Anger flickered across his dark eyes.

"Miss, I'd appreciate you showing me some respect."

He brought his hands to fists, so tightly his knuckles turned white. The movement made him sweat more. It made Declan squirm in his seat.

"Unfortunately, a girl is missing."

He stood up leaning over the desk. His face turned a deep red. His eyes blazing with anger.

"I AM THE MAYOR. YOU WILL GIVE ME RESPECT"

His booming voice echoed throughout the office. She was winding him up like the old toys. This time it didn't take long. Jessica stood and met his gaze.

"Respect has to be earned."

"YOU'RE JUST LIKE THAT BITCH ROSE, SHE DID QUIT AFTER SCREWING EVERYTHING UP."

Jessica's rage built up inside. Her hands tensed on the edge of the desk.

Declan stood up and put his hand on Jessica's shoulder, lightly pulling her back. The Mayor moved back too. He gulped down the rest of his drink and pushed aggressively on a button under the desk. Within a moment the door swung open. The woman from before stood in the open frame. The man composed himself and calmed his voice.

"Yes, sir."

"Escort the detectives out."

She nodded, taking Declan and Jessica out of the office. She shut the door. Jessica could see the silhouette of the Mayor pacing in his office. The woman walked them over to the top of the stairs. Then she stopped and turned to face Jessica.

"You're here about Rose, aren't you?"

"Did you know her?"

A man walked past and smiled at the woman. Once he left, she looked around nervously. Then whispered,

"I can't talk now. Meet me at the cafe on the corner at one thirty."

Jessica nodded. The bell sounded at the woman's desk again. She smiled and rushed back into the Mayor's office.

Jessica and Declan sat in the cafe, waiting until one thirty. The young waitress walked over to the table. She was wearing a short red dress that stopped just at the top of her thighs. Declan ordered a glass of water. Jessica glanced down at the menu and ordered a tea. The street was silent. Jessica saw the waitress carrying the drinks. She nodded that she had the right table. She raised her eyebrows and put the glasses down.

They saw the woman racing down the street.

She sat down opposite the detectives and pulled the ashtray over to her. She pulled a Benson&Hedges blue cigarette box from her pocket placing one on her lips and pulled it from the plastic lining. She searched through her pockets and pulled out a thin box of lighters from a local strip club. She flicked it open and saw it was empty. She took out her cigarette and held it between her fingers. Her lips were lightly dyed with yellow tar. Jessica met her stare and smiled.

"Do any of you have a light?"

Declan reached in his pocket and pulled out a silver lighter. He flicked the flint and sparked a blue flame. The flame flickered slightly in the wind. He reached across the table. The woman put the end of the fag into the flame and burnt off the excess paper.

"I don't have long."

"That's fine; just tell me what you know."

The woman breathed in the smoke of the cigarette blowing it out into the air. The grey ash fell lightly onto the table. The woman brushed it off with the back off her hand.

38

"Rose was lovely; she worked very hard until a few weeks ago she started making mistakes with finance reports, if I asked what was wrong, she wouldn't answer."

She tapped the tip of the fag into the ashtray. The ash flickered as it fell into the glass tray. She took another heavy drag of the cigarette and coughed as the smoke hit her lungs.

"Then last week a woman came to the office I think her name was Crystal, she went to see the Mayor. After she left, I heard the Mayor shouting at Rose. She left crying. After that when she was on shift she was angry and always in a rush."

Declan sipped his water; the ice rattled against the sides of the glass. The woman crossed her legs, started fiddling with her long fringe.

"Do you have any idea what happened with Crystal?"

Jessica chose her words carefully she had no idea what she knew if anything about the case. Declan pulled a notebook and pen from the inside pocked of his jacket. And flipped it open on the table.

"Look, you can't tell anyone I told you any of this."

"We won't but we need to find Rose."

"The Mayor makes regular payments to a company called Dream Desires. After the visit, the payments increased until they just stopped."

"How do you know this?"

The woman pushed her cigarette into the ashtray, the end flooding over and burning out. She picked up the red napkin and whipped harshly across her lips. Declan's eyes widened.

"Once Rose left, I was brought in to replace her, I found the person's finance report on her desk."

She unfolded a piece of paper form her bag and slid it over to the detectives. She looked at her watch and pulling out a thick tube of lipstick. She applied it thickly to her lips and wiped off the small line of excess. Jessica saw the moisture on her lips shine and her mind raced back to Ava. Declan said nothing, just stared down at the table in front of him.

"I have to go."

The woman stood and walked away from the table her heels clicking against the pavement. She turned back and picked up Declan's water. She drank down all the water leaving only the ice and winked across at Declan. He winked back and slid the paper across the table. The woman walked off. Declan watched her legs as she walked.

Declan read the sheet of paper. Pressing it out onto the glass table.

"She was right, they have made monthly payments to Dream Desires until two weeks ago."

Jessica swallowed down the rest of her tea and unwrapped the ginger biscuit.

They left and drove to the Dream Desires office. Traffic was heavy going back into the centre. Declan lowered the car window to let in the fresh air. Twenty minutes later, they pulled into a small industrial estate. The address was a one-storey building a mile east of the town hall. After driving up to the door Jessica parked on the curb outside, and she and Declan got out. The building was grey and basic. Declan saw the sign hanging above the door:

Dream Desires.
Company for VIP members
Enquire within.

Jessica punched the first button. It was listed as 'Reception.' The other buttons had been covered with black tape.

"Welcome to Dream Desires. You are here about the job? If you could just give me your name."

Jessica noticed the small lens at the top. Hidden behind the pinprick hole at the top.

"Police, open up."

She pulled her badge out and showed it to the camera. A moment later the door buzzed and she pushed through it.

The office was a large open room, lined with black metal desks. Jessica walked down the thin isle between each one. Declan followed. There was a small office right at the end. Jessica knocked hard on the glass door. There was no answer for nearly three minutes. Declan pointed to the painted silhouette on the wall. His eyes followed the features of the naked woman. He loosened his tie slightly as he turned back to Jessica. They could be so much more but no one ever told them. Jessica felt sorry for the women. But she couldn't think about it for too long. A woman looked through the window and frowned. She swung open the door. She was on the phone, she gestured the detectives in. She hung up and put her phone down on the desk.

"What do you want? I had a permit for all my girls."

"We're only here about one girl, Crystal."

"Oh you found her. Tell her she still owes me."

"Crystal is missing. We came to ask her some questions about her clientele."

"She was called over to see her regulars but this time she took the money and ran off."

Jessica leaned forward. The woman walked over to a printer and took some pages from the tray.

Jessica had been ready for about anything. But she wasn't ready for that.

"Was her client the Mayor?"

"I can't say, client confidentiality."

"Have you ever heard the name Rose Nunez?"

"She was here a few weeks ago about Crystal's regular client and what he paid for. She had the nerve to call me disgusting."

"What did she want to know?"

"Where Crystal lived?"

"Did you tell her?"

"She threatened to expose something that would shut us down. I had no choice, I told her."

"Where does Crystal live?"

"She rents a room at the Blackened Hill Casino hotel."

She stood and walked to the door. She reached for the handle as she spoke.

"Please keep my company out of your investigation."

Jessica got up from the table and headed for the door. She looked directly at the woman when she mentioned her company and said as if money was the only thing she cared about.

"I can't promise that."

She stepped out and closed the door.

Declan wrapped hard on the door for the fourth time. There was no answer. He pushed down on the handle. She closed the door. Then pulled off the chain and opened it again. Not to make a forced entry, she put her gun in the holster.

He could see a pale arm stretched out at the foot of the bed. The room was upturned from the struggle. A smashed glass lay at the foot of the door. He pulled back and swathed hard on his stubble. Jessica looked to see the hand and pushed against the door, snapping the chain off its hinge. She walked fully into the room. Declan stepped on an empty condom packet. Durex ribbed. He remembered the line from the adverts:

For her pleasure

Thinking about it made him want to throw up. The metal ashtray was filled with blunt cigarettes and spliffs. The odour totally filled the room. He saw the body. Jessica stepped closer to the sofa, her hands on her knees, looking at the body. She was disgusted. Declan walked over to the desk and flicked off the humming fan. Forcing the room into silence.

The woman's body lay on the fur rug. The white fabric was stained with brown, dried blood. Her mouth was open and blood was pooled in it.

The contents of her purse were scattered next to the body. Jessica reached down to pick up a business card from under the bed. The front of the card depicted the naked woman silhouette from the Dream Desires office. She flipped it over and read the back:

Cristal Waters
Company for the VIP.
Dream Desires.

The name was spelt wrong. Jessica realised Crystal probably couldn't read. Jessica shook her head once. Another dead hooker. She realised they couldn't track the clients. In that business they usually pay cash.

Jessica turned and looked off at the view. She didn't want to look at the girl anymore. She felt a pang of sadness. It seemed too much of a coincidence that all the cases were connected.

Deciding she had seen enough, she took the elevator down to the ground floor. She went out the front and waited on the bench across the street. She decided to smoke while she waited for Watts to finish.

She waited and watched the building. Watts came out and pulled his bag strap over his shoulder, ready to leave. He walked over to Jessica and threw himself down onto the seat. His face was drained of blood. He stared off into the distance until he snapped back to Jessica.

"There's no official cause of death yet but I'm betting it was a fixation."

Jessica turned back to him. His eyes lowered as he considered things.

"What about physical evidence?"

"I'm afraid whoever did this was a pro; place was wiped clean."

Jessica chewed the edge of her nails. A question burned in her head. Had Rose found the murderer and been silenced?

Jessica sat at the counter at the All-press espresso bar and drank a coffee, eating a plate of pancakes covered in syrup. She had a notebook open on the counter. She felt depressed. She couldn't get Ava out of her head. The rain began to sleet against the window. Jessica looked into her empty mug; black bits of coffee were stuck to the bottom. She signalled over to the waitress with her mug and waited for another coffee. Jessica could hear and smell the food being cooked. It made her stomach pang. This was the first thing she had eaten in days. She looked down at the open sugar, hoping it would tell her something. A couple of teenagers stood up and left. Jessica looked towards where they had been. There was an empty liqueur bag on the table. Just another set of fake IDs. Looking at the empty bag made Jessica yearn for a drink. But it wasn't a game she wanted to play again.

The bell above the chime sounded. It told the staff someone was coming in She still faced the door. Her stomach dropped. Ava walked into the café. She approached and waited for Jessica to look up. Her hair was tied behind her head and she wore green emerald earrings. For a moment no one said anything. Jessica leaned back and tried to think of what to say. But only managed a nod.

"Well?"

Jessica looked at her with eyes that could've carved steel. Ava's face turned blotchy, kind of pink and white.

"Well what?"

Ava bent down close to her face. They were both silent for a few moments. There was something about Ava she couldn't reach.

She never took her eyes off Ava in the room. Jessica felt the guilt pass over her. She knew it was wrong of course. She wasn't thinking right.

Jessica left the café and walked out onto the street. Jessica wanted to leave. To go somewhere and think about things. She lit a cigarette and crossed over the street. The street was quiet and empty—it had a ghostly feel. At any moment you expected to see the dead walking towards you.

It was lined with old shops and abandoned buildings. Ava met her by her car. Jessica turned to walk away. Ava dug her clipped nails painlessly into Jessica hand.

She studied her face. She had flecks of green in her eyes. She ran her hands down her neck and over her earrings, her skin was soft and warm.

Jessica conceded and let her use her body the way she wanted. She watched silently as Ava walked towards her. Her tongue slightly slid out of her mouth and licked across her lip. Jessica smiled and let the lust burn through her body. It was the strongest thing she'd felt in years.

"You're loving this, aren't you?"

She took another drag from her cigarette. Liking the yellow stain from her lips.

"You got me."

Ava said. Jessica's gaze focused as Ava's face leaned close and kissed her. Her finger hovered along Jessica's belt line feeling the gun. Her abs tensed with the touch.

Her heartbeat rapidly increased and she felt the rush of blood. It had been so many years since she felt this alive. But she pulled back and willed her legs to move.

"I don't want to do this."

47

Ava just nodded. But the words handed a heavy blow. Jessica was silent for a moment. She didn't want to speak. Ava forced a smile to ease her.

With that, Ava turned around and headed back to her car, and started it up. Jessica stepped back to the door and flicked the butt out.

She opened her eyes and leaned forward.

She looked at her drive away; for a moment, she felt sorry for her mistake.

Jessica had a surprise waiting for her when she arrived at the crime scene. It was quarter to seven in the morning. She realised she hadn't slept for over seventy-two hours—God she was tired. There were hundreds of people already crowded into the space. Declan came over. The wind had forced his clothes to cling to his muscular figure. He handed her the end of a cigarette as she stepped from the car.

"Do you want to kill that?"

Jessica nodded and took it. She took three long drags and stumped it out. Declan noticed Watt's period mustang wasn't there. He hitched his shoulders as if it unsettled him. Jessica brushed her hand through her hair as she stepped towards the body.

Fog filled the street and looked like a smoke screen hiding something dark. She followed Declan over to the side of the nearest building. The body had been propped against the wall. He was stripped completely naked. She thought about it. She wondered if it was hard for the Angel to remove his clothes. Was he forced to take them off first? But the blow at the back of his head meant he was probably unconscious by then.

He was chained to the drainpipe by his right arm. His skin was red and bruised. She walked over crouching down examining the different marks. Then she saw his chest move up and down. She pressed her fingers against his cold neck. He had a pulse.

"Declan, he's still alive."

Declan raced over and felt the faint pulse in the man's neck.

"CHRIST!"

The man came to. His face looked painted but his eyes were still bright.

"Where am I?"

"I'm Detective Denning, the ambulance is on its way."

The blue and red lights flashed through the thick fog. Two men ran over, putting the man on a long stretcher. Jessica looked back down at the scene. She saw a small movement on the wall. She shined her torch, a circle of light illuminating a piece of paper pinned to the wall. She pulled it off the wind almost blowing it from her hands.

The cursive writing shined from the streetlight as the ink was still wet.

The waiting room had three rows of plastic chairs, all pointing to the nurse's station. Almost all the chairs were taken; each person waited patiently to hear about their loved ones. Jessica crammed herself between two people. The old man on the left rested his head against her shoulder and fell asleep. Jessica didn't mind. She found his breathing calming. Underneath the chair was the newest addition of hot celeb magazine. The cover was a grainy image of a celebrity. They had blurred out her face but left her bare, plastic filled chest. She imagined the humiliation of the actress when she brought the magazine home. She put the magazine back under the chair. A nurse came and sat next to her interrupting her thoughts. She was dark and beautiful and had a mature smile. She retained her beauty but worry lines had craved away at her face and her eyes lost some of their brightness.

"Detective Denning, Dale Archers is awake you can see him now."

They walked through the hallway that branched left and right. Jessica followed the nurse to a large room with several beds. Two uniformed officers stood at the edge of the nearest bed. She noticed a man standing by the door with a holster on his waistband—another detective. Jessica held up her open badge. He waved her on. She sat on the chair next to the bed facing Dale Archer.

The sun was high in the sky and Jessica could feel its warmth through the glass. Blood had already seeped through his bandages and onto the bed. Most of his face was covered in blood and bruises.

But Jessica could see his eyes. They still had regret and sadness—but mostly pain. He looked almost haunted.

"Why don't you tell me about Rose Nunez?"

She looked at him as though she could read his sadness. His eyes seemed to look into hers.

"Mr Archer, if I leave you without you telling me anything, the Angel will find you again."

His facade broke, and like a delicate glass structure, revealed a timid and weak child-like man beneath.

"Then I'm a dead man either way."

"We can offer protection."

"Not from them."

"From who? Mr Archer, tell me."

"I assume you already know, I was hired by the Mayor's office."

Jessica nodded and sat further back in the chair. Like a child, she felt a tinge of excitement.

"I was given the order to kill Rose Nunez."

"Why didn't you say no?"

Jessica realised his face showed fear and loneliness. He was just another victim of Francis Jaeger.

"They find you when you're young. When you're alone. But they groom you to be something you never wanted to be. They make you into something you fear."

He shut his eyes and let the blackness swarm around him. He breathed deep into the dark. Breathing it back into his lungs.

"I can get him. But I need you."

He looked at her as if he had never heard those words before.

"There are worst things to fear than death. What they do is much worse."

"Who would do this?"

"I'm no saint but he, he is evil and he knows too much."

"Just tell me who he is."

"You're going to find her body. I killed her because I was afraid. I killed her because I didn't know what else to do."

His cheeks were wet with tears as he pulled himself up on the bed. He groaned at the pain in his chest as he slid a crucifix across the bed. Jessica knew instantly it was the one that belonged to Rose.

They looked at each other. Then Jessica stepped closer. He pulled her close and wrapped his arms around. He finished his story by saying,

"He told me the people I killed were only ever bad people; people who deserved it."

"Rose didn't deserve to die."

He grabbed the gun and tore it from the holster. Within a second, he pushed the barrel to the back of his throat and pulled the trigger. Jessica leapt forward and grabbed his head as it fell. His finger shook as it released. His hands flew from the shotgun and slammed down against the edge of the bed. His face disappeared into the darkness. She brought her hand up to cover her mouth.

London Motel One was located opposite the roundabout on Trafalgar road. As she drove she opened the window fully and bathed her face in the dry air. The sign advertised free Wi-Fi, colour television, as though no one else offered those things. The motel was as the name suggested—one of the last—but that wasn't the first thing you noticed. The first thing you noticed was the off-white colour of the walls. Motel One was the kind of seedy and dirty place that made you want to wash your whole body.

Jessica pushed the door to the bedroom open with her foot. She saw drops of blood on the floor. She hit the door handle with her hip. It only opened about an inch or so. There was something on the other side holding it closed. Jessica put her coffee down on the bed and pushed all her weight against the door. It slowly moved opened as the blockage gave way. She squeezed through and saw a table had been shoved against the door. She was standing in the alley behind the room and the morning traffic surged past the entrance. Each driver glanced down at the scene, wondering what was happening.

The wind was blowing the rubbish around.

"Fuck."

Jessica turned. It was Watts and he was combing his hair over with a brush. Pulling out the wiry white hair.

"Excuse me?"

"The camera really does love me."

He pulled out his phone and looked at his reflection on the blank screen. The coroner looked at him from under his overgrown eyebrows.

"Watts show some respect."

He nodded down at the body. He smoothed back his eyebrows and pocketed his phone. There was a long silence. Watts reluctantly gave the coroner another nod, exhaled and moved towards the body.

"I guess you recognise the victim?"

Jessica looked at the damaged face for a long moment before saying.

"Shit! It's Nunez."

Watts nodded as he zipped up the body bag. Jessica looked down at her watch. It was nearly seven-thirty. The moon had already vaguely risen in the sky.

"How long has she been dead?"

"About two weeks but she was only dumped here last night."

The coroner said,

"Any other DNA?"

"No, the body's been wiped clean. The only thing I can tell you for now is she was frozen after her death."

"Does that tell us anything about who killed her?"

"The burns on her arms and legs suggest it was a large conventional freezer found in businesses."

He picked up the victim's arm showing Jessica the red swollen burns.

The Cuban-American man sat at her desk. His leg frantically twitched against the steel chair.

"Mr Nunez."

Jessica said. He looked up at her.

"Detective Denning, you found my wife? Is she okay?"

The desperation in his voice was heart-breaking. A searing bolt of pain travelled to his head.

"I'm sorry Mr Nunez, we found your wife's body this morning—she had been killed."

The man dropped to the floor, tears streamed from his jaded eyes. He screamed in agony. She guided him to the break room and left him with Declan. She couldn't deal with it, she knew that pain. Clayton was waiting outside the door.

"Detective Denning, have you questioned the husband yet?"

He was looking at his phone as he spoke, a smile swept across his thin lips. Jessica pulled at her lips and pushed the memories back down again.

"I'm about to go back in, sir."

Jessica leaned to the door and opened it. Before entering she turned and watched Clayton as he read the file which was open on her desk. She stepped into the room and closed the door behind her.

"Mr Nunez, would you be able to answer some questions?"

The table was covered in soaked tissues.

"Of course, anything for Rose."

"We believe your wife was murdered."

His face dropped at the word 'murder'.

"Can you think of anyone who would want to hurt Rose?"

He paused for a long moment before he spoke.

"No. No one."

"Are you sure?"

"The man who killed her shot himself last night, he told us someone had hired him."

Anger flickered across his eyes. Jessica reached for the evidence bag on the chair. The man looked up at her confused.

"I thought you would want this back."

He looked at the bag as though it held an answer.

"Can I take it out?"

"Of course."

He gently fingered the thin, gold chain and pressed hard on the engraved cross. He brought it up to his lips so he could taste the cold metal.

"Please can I see my wife?"

He kept his eyes on the cross while he spoke.

"You will need to identify the body."

The man nodded and followed Jessica out of the door.

Jessica pushed the office chair in front of the monitor and turned on the CCTV footage. She watched as drunks swayed across the screen. She stopped it as she saw Rose turning the corner. Her finger rested above the mouse. She didn't want to see it but she knew she didn't have a choice. She rubbed the edge of her phone against her cheek as she thought about it.

The image of the killer was grainy and blurred. She opened the enhanced image from the tech guys.

And that was when she noticed the watch. It was a Rolex— one of the ones with the twisted bands. She couldn't see the face but she wrote down what she had. His height, weight and expensive watch.

She snapped on her iPod, letting the music calm her while she watched. It didn't work. The songs just added a background to what was happening. She tried to change the music and chose something happier but it just felt insulting.

She watched carefully as Rose tore around the corner the look of sheer terror on her face. All the colour had gone from her face. She stared down at the image on the screen and felt a sharp pang of guilt.

"I've got something for you, and I think you're going to like it."

"Go on."

"The Mayor's financial showed that two weeks ago, he hired a bodyguard from the Blackened Hill Casino."

Jessica smiled and slammed the laptop shut.

"Do we have a name?"

"He hired Dale Archer, I ran the DNA against other crimes."

He reached behind and grabbed a file off his desk.

"Dale Archer was questioned in connection with the murder of Archie Rimland."

"Who was lead?"

"DCI David Leigh."

Jessica stood on the porch and knocked hard on the door. There was no answer. The thick curtains were drawn and blocked out all the natural light. She reached up and tried the bell. A rasp and harsh voice called from behind the door.

"What do you want?"

Jessica heard the sound of him loading a gun. She pulled out her gun and held it close to her hip. The cold metal pressed into her thigh.

"My name is Detective Jessica Denning. I need you to put down your weapon DCI Leigh."

The door opened and cast a dark strip of shadow on the flagstones.

"Show me your badge."

She grabbed her badge and presented it through the crack in the door.

DCI Leigh swung the door fully open. A cloud of dust billowed out and the smell of tobacco filled the clean air.

She dropped the gun to the side and entered. The place was as dark as night.

The hallway was small and consumed by dark wallpaper and unclean carpet. There was a bookcase with a radio in it. BBC3 was on. Jessica's eyes adjusted to the darkness. DCI Leigh shut the door and turned to look at Jessica. He saw the gun resting on her hip.

"You can put that away, I just wanted to see who you were."

He pointed his pale hand down to a table by the door. The gun lay on the varnished surface. Jessica hesitated but finally holstered her gun and followed Leigh into the sitting room.

Leigh slumped into one of the big chairs and brought his back above his head.

"Have a seat, Detective."

Jessica ignored it and stayed standing.

"I take it you heard Dale Archer committed suicide last night."

"Yes, I heard something about it on the radio."

"You must have recognised the name from the Rimland case."

She could feel his eyes burning through her.

"Memory's not what it used to be."

"Archie Rimland was the 14-year-old boy who was taken and murdered. Alone and terrified."

He grimaced at her words. They handed a heavy blow.

"You need to let that go—it's over—nothing more to be done."

"With all due respect sir, there is more to be done. I am currently leading an investigation into the brutal murder of Rose Nunez. Dale Archer was the person who killed her."

Leigh finally came away from his thoughts and looked at Jessica.

"You were the only one to leave his files and photograph in the case notes, why?"

"They told me it would end if I just did as they say. But I wasn't stupid. I knew they were lying. I just hoped I was wrong."

"Who told you?"

"I'm an old man now and I have lived with this guilt upon me for all these years, because I was afraid."

"We can offer protection."

"You will try but it's okay, I have to make peace with my demons, and that case was the worst of my career. The poor boy had been disregarded as nothing."

He started to cry. Jessica didn't know what to do. Comforting him would be wrong.

"I found Archer's name on a list of contacts from the parents. Something about child-care for a holiday."

"What happened? Archer was never even questioned."

"He was brought in for questioning but the case was overruled by a superior officer."

Jessica was silent. She didn't know what to say.

"The Chief informed my team they had found some DNA evidence on the body that identified the killer."

"You should have been in charge of DNA."

The man nodded.

"The chief had apparently found a piece of evidence that had been seized but never sent to the lab."

"Who was sentenced?"

"No one. The man whose DNA was found on Archie Rimland's body was a convicted paedophile who was killed by the community where he lived."

"Was there any sign of sexual assault?"

Leigh shook his head. It was not a sex-filled crime. Made a change.

"The pathologist ruled there was no sign of sexual activity on the boy."

It didn't make any sense.

"What was the DNA found?"

"Semen on Archie's shirt."

"Didn't you question it?"

He looked angry and hurt by her words.

"Of course. But when I took my concerns to the deputy chief constable I was offered senior position to keep quiet."

Jessica's jaw fell open.

"He told me about a man who arranged it all. Who could make my dark fantasies real."

Jessica waited a moment. The next question was crucial.

"Who?"

"Francis Jaeger, the owner of the Blackened Hill Casino."

Tear tracks ran down his cheeks.

"One more thing detective, don't be afraid or he will feed on your fear."

DCI Leigh watched her drive off through his window. He walked back to the cabinet in that hall and grabbed his gun. Sitting back down in the chair. He pushed the barrel up to his temple feeling the cold metal against his kin and pulled the trigger. The gun fell across the floor and landed on the rug. He wouldn't fail anyone else.

The sun set at eight twenty-one in the evening.

Jessica's car phone buzzed and she saw it was Declan. As she answered, she closed the window thinking it was a private call.

Jessica ended the call. She changed the brightness to see the screen. The screen lit and on the display was a photo DCI Leigh. She cast a wistful look at the photo. Staring with damp brown eyes. She felt another pang of guilt.

Jessica leaned down close towards the screen. There was a single bullet hole in the side of his head. His eyes looked cold and hollow. His skull was shattered leaving his face badly misshapen.

His eyes were puffy from recent tears. The face wasn't bloated from crying. The place was as grey as stone.

The image made Jessica want to puke. She looked at the photo for a long moment before moving.

To rid some of her ease, she let her mind wander to drink and started thinking about it all. Some days she couldn't be above doing it.

She walked down the hall to the fridge and found a can of old Grouse Cider. She stared at it for a moment and then swiftly moved back to her seat. She let out a deep breath of frustration. She would have pondered it further, except for a knock and suddenly the front door opened. She had forgotten to lock it. Ava was waiting on the worn welcome mat with a smile. She hadn't bothered to get rid of the dust since she moved in.

"Can I come in?"

Jessica nodded.

"Come on in."

Ava let the door close as she walked inside. She felt the great early attraction when she looked at Jessica. She swallowed hard. Ava lowered her gaze.

Jessica couldn't help it; she crumbled under the weight of her guilt burying her head in her hands. Tears filled her cupped palms. She felt the cushion next to her dip under the weight of Ava. She felt a warm soft hand stroke across her back and the other gently stroking her along thighs and pulled her into a sensitive embrace. Jessica was hit with her soft lavender perfume. Her heart jumped in her chest as the smell swam through her blood.

"What's wrong, Jessica?"

Jessica didn't answer. She just sat very still.
Ava leaned forward and lowered her head into her hands.

"What's wrong?"

Ava asked again. Jessica answered by asking her own question. Her wistful smile stayed in place.

"Why did you come here?"

"I wanted to see you."

A smile spread across Jessica face. Ava leaned back in the chair.

"I don't want to tell you. I'm protecting you."

"That's not good enough, Ava. Tell me."

The question made her heart slam into her throat.

More silence. Jessica could see she was thinking. She crossed her arms and tried to look angry. She tightened her lips before answering.

"Fine. If you really want to know."

She frowned as though Jessica was putting her in a difficult position.

The chair creaked with the movement as she bent forward and pulled up her shirt around her neck.

Jessica helped her lift her top and ran her finger down the raised scars. Her skin was warm and red. Jessica stared at her for a long moment and Ava quickly grew uncomfortable.

"The man pulled me up to face him. He had such evil in his eyes. I reached across and felt a small broken bit of pipe next to me. I grabbed it and thrust it into his stomach over and over. I wasn't helpless anymore. I loved that feeling."

She spoke in monotone.

Ava stared down at the floor and Jessica wondered if she was replaying the memory. She felt the crushing guilt. The Fallen Angel was born from a dire situation. In that incident, she had fallen from grace after having her wings torn from her back and her innocence stolen as with each plunge of the pipe, part of her halo fell shattering around her like shards of glass. Her back arched at the memories. She couldn't move.

Jessica smiled though Ava couldn't see it. Ava smiled— it was her way of telling Jessica she was okay.

Ava left and slammed the door shut behind her. Jessica's mind raced and she realised she hadn't handled it very well. She grabbed the pouch of Amber Leaf off the bedside table and rolled a cigarette. She sat on the balcony outside her bedroom with the unlit cigarette between her lips. She was about to light it when she heard a knock at the door. She quickly stood up and threw the cigarette onto the fire escape. She swung back in and answered the door. It was Ava Dowler.

"Ava, hello."

"Can I come in?"

"Of course."

She moved to the side and let her in. Ava looked around and saw the open window above the bed. Jessica spoke first.

"What are you doing back here?"

"I wanted to see you and apologise for before."

She slipped her coat off. Beads of rain clung to the fabric. She was wearing a flowing black dress. Cut just above her knee.

"It's okay, I understand I didn't handle it very well."

She smiled at her, eyes burning with lust.

"You got any more of those."

She nodded her head towards the empty beer bottles next to the sofa.

"In the fridge."

Ava walked over from the fridge carrying two iced beers. Her hair was neatly scraped behind her head. It reminded Jessica of her teachers at school. Apart from the single wisp of blonde hair that had fallen across her face. She passed a bottle across to Jessica and pressed one to her own lips. Jessica reached across for the bottle and took a quick sip. Ava's eyes stayed firmly on Jessica's. She took another sip and licked off the moisture from her lips.

"Do you want a glass for that?"

"No there aren't any clean."

Ava glanced across at the dishes piled up on the kitchen sink.

"Spending a lot of time away then."

Jessica nodded and took another sip of her beer. She let her eyes track down Ava's dress.
Ava walked over to Jessica and kissed her lips. Jessica dropped her beer onto the floor. The remains spilled out across the carpet. She laughed and wrapped her arms tightly around Ava.

They pressed against each other and moved towards the bedroom. Ava reached across and put her beer down on the table so she could have both hands free as they tore at each other's clothes. Jessica threw Ava's dress across the room and ran her hands down her scars. Ava groaned as she shut out the memories and pushed Jessica down onto the bed. They made love. It was long and passionate. But it satisfied the burning lust Jessica had felt.

When it was over, Jessica lay on top of Ava. Her fist still entwined in her hair. The sheets were sprawled beneath them. Ava reached across and grabbed her bottle from beside the bed. She drank down what was left and dropped the bottle down next to the bed.

Jessica worked her way down and lay on Ava's chest.

"What was that for then?"

Jessica said as Ava stroked softly down her back.

"Because I wanted to."

She looked down and smiled, showing her white teeth. They were so straight, Jessica knew she had worn braces. That thought made her smile. She began running her hands through Ava's hair. They were both being much softer now. Ava continued to softly run down her back. Jessica smirked and held back a laugh in her throat.

"What do you mean?"

"After everything, I realised how much I wanted you."

Jessica lifted her head up and stared at Ava. Her eyes were wide and tired. Ava looked across at the still open window.

She swung the thick duvet over them. Jessica looked up at her again and reached for her phone. She quickly took a photo while Ava was looking away.

"What?"

Ava smiled down at her and nodded towards the window.

"No wonder it's so cold."

Jessica swung over and cuddled into the covers. Ava turned over and kissed her and got up out of the bed. Jessica pulled herself up and rested against the headboard.

Ava gathered up her clothes and walked over to the window. She shut and locked it.

"The clean towels are in the airing cupboard."

Jessica said. She insisted Ava took a shower first and she did. Jessica jumped into the shower straight after and let the scorching water run over her body. She breathed in heavily so she could still smell Ava's soft perfume on her skin. Ava was sitting at the dining table as Jessica came out of the bathroom fully dressed. She looked at the two cups of steaming coffee and smiled. She sat down and was silent for a moment while they sipped there coffee.

They were both trying to figure out what the last few hours meant for them.

"What are you thinking about?"

"What happens next?"

"Maybe we should just see how it plays out."

That didn't sound the same as what had just happened between them. Ava shifted in her seat and stood up. Jessica stood up and joined her.

"I better go."

"Where are you going?"

"Back to the station to see what's going on."

"What's happening with your case?"

"Nothing really, this is a tough one."

Jessica walked towards the door and Ava followed. Leaving the beer stain soaking into the carpet. She pulled the door closed for her.

"Where's your car, Ava?"

"Just down the street."

"I'll walk you over."

When they reached the car, Ava turned to face Jessica. Jessica's mind was still stuck firmly on the case.

"I want to get this guy," she said, "more than anything."

Ava moved close and kissed her. Her voice was a whisper.

"You will."

She leaned in to kiss her again. Jessica pulled back.

"Knock it off."

Ava playfully whispered into her ear and bit down harsh on the lobe. The sharp pain caused a rush of air to push from Jessica's body.

"No."

She leaned forward and kissed her again. She smiled and then got into the car. Jessica walked back over to her building and got into her car. She thought of her brother. The one person she wanted to tell but couldn't. Her mind wandered to her night with Ava.

Jessica had just gotten back to the station with a stack of files under her arm.

The door to the Chiefs office opened and Jessica walked in. The Deputy Chief Constable Harry Clayton rested on the edge of the desk. He always wore a tight fitted suit. That was the first thought that crossed Jessica's mind. His eyes were dark and cold as they watched her walk towards him. Harry was a huge man, but when cut down he was weak and timid. They fell into silence for a moment. She saw his chest hitch, as he felt the pressure of the situation.

"Detective Denning, please sit down."

She sat on the metal chair in front of Clayton.

"What can I do for you, sir?"

"I'm a very busy man, so I'll get straight to the point. Francis Jaeger is a very influential man."

"I understand, sir, but…"

"Good. Leave the Blackened Hill Casino out of your investigation. I like the husband for this, he is controlling."

"Sir, I have to follow the evidence."

He stood and walked to the door.

"Leave Francis Jaeger out or I'll take you off homicide."

He pushed down on the handle and opened the door.

"Wait sir, why?"

He smiled smugly and grunted under his breath.

"I think you know why."

He left. Jessica looked down at her hands; they were red from the tightness of her grip. She walked over to the desk and poured herself a glass of water. She felt the spike of fear stab in her chest. Declan swung open the door and walked over to Jessica.

"I've reviewed the case the Angel was wanted for."

She sipped the water and put the glass back down on the desk.

"Did you find anything?"

"Five yards against the first case involving the Angel was investigated."

"What happened?"

"A sixteen-year-old named Joe Dowler was arrested for GBH and assault with diminished responsibility against Howard Jaeger. When he was released he was attacked by Howard and his bodyguard, the vigilante killed the attackers and saved him."

"How did they know it was the Angel?"

"They found a note on one of the bodies."

She followed Declan out of the office. Her hands were still shaking from her meeting with Clayton.

It had started to rain. Jessica pulled into the street and shut off her car.

She started further into the house. Jessica went in through the kitchen. She walked down the hallway and leaned close to the closed bedroom door. She reached for the knob and slowly opened the door. She flicked the wall switch and a lamp in the corner came on. The place was quiet, only the sound of the rain on the roof. She looked through the doors onto the bed and from that angle saw something at the top. She stepped over to the bed and flicked on another light. There were three green beer bottles lined up on the floor. She turned to the side and there lying across the pillows was Rose Nunez's body. Blood was splattered on the pillow above her head and up the wall. Her blonde hair was knotted and unclean. She stepped closer. Rose's mouth was open and drowning in blood. She took a step back to the stool at the end of the bed and saw a pistol lying on the floor. She looked back at the woman's body.

There was a three-inch exit hole in her left temple.

Jessica watched Watts close the bag over Rose's face while two others helped lift her onto the gurney. They covered her in a black sheet and wheeled her out through the house to the front door. Jessica turned. Declan was beckoning her from the hallway. Jessica went inside and followed Declan to the living room. The coroner was already standing there.

She looked out onto the balcony.

Two uniforms were leaned against it puffing heavily on their straight cigarettes. Stanley Watts said very little to the uniforms as he walked back into the house. He was a short man with thin hair which he had a bald spot which he covered with a whispery comb over. He was getting old.

"Bullet to the head."

He stood up and shook his head. Jessica looked away from Watts and tried to contain the anger that was burning inside. The coroner and Watts held each other's stares.

He pulled of his leather gloves and stroked the back of his neck with his bony fingers.

"How long has she been dead?"

Jessica asked. She stepped back, folding her hands and putting a hard expression on her face. It didn't match her features.

"Couple of hours at the most."

"That's right. Now I know some of us haven't had any sleep but I got a hot blonde in my bed at home. So I best get going."

Watts winked and Jessica and let his hand fall down to his crotch.

"FUCK OFF, WATTS!"

Declan moved off to stop the anger taking over him. Watt's flipped his middle finger up at Declan and stepped back into the doorframe. Declan fired up his e-cigarette, breathing a cloud of smoke into the air.
"Thanks."

Jessica put her hand on the coroner's shoulder. He had been here since she joined homicide but she knew he was close to giving it up.

As they drove down Marlborough road, Declan rolled down the window and watched the cars in the traffic. His phone rang in his pocket. His upper thigh told him it was a call rather than a text.

"Detective Hughes."

"Detective I have the statement from Mary Talbert's said parents."

"Was there anything?"

"I found a link between Mary's case and Rose Nunez."

Declan put the phone on speaker and rested it on the dashboard.

"Mary Talbert worked at the Blackened Hill Casino during her final year of university. It is the same casino that the hitmen were hired from to kill Rose. Mary was fired the day before she was killed."

He hung up and looked over at Jessica. She flicked on her sirens and turned the car around heading to the Blackened Hill Casino.

Declan followed Jessica through the doors into the casino. The whole place was designed to take away your senses. Instantly, she was blinded by the bright lights. The air was filled with winner's screams. He walked up to the desk at the end of the open room.

Declan captured the woman's attention. He always stood out. He was special and it bothered him. Jessica looked at him; he looked like he'd aged years in last week. He forced a smile for her. Most people assumed they were together. Declan thought it bothered Jessica—it didn't.

The woman behind the desk gave him a toothy smile and showed her pierced lip. Jessica recognised her face from high school. She remembered her being known as the school slut.

She still looked the same, smiled the same and acted the same. She even wore the same cheap perfume.

"How much would you like to change today? I live to serve you."

Her voice drifted off. She swept her hair behind her ear. The speakers played eighties hits. The walls were covered in sun-faded photos of celebrities.

"You went to Regent High, Jessica isn't it?"

"It's Detective Denning now."

"Wow. What about Luke?"

Jessica heart dropped.

"I need to see Francis Jaeger."

Jessica slammed her badge down onto the glass. The girl did a startled jump. Her short skirt rose up when she stood. She was still wearing fishnet stockings. They had torn at the top of her thighs. The girl Jessica used to call a 'floozy – big-boobed, blonde and brainless'. She was the same as the fourteen-year old version. She said nothing and waited. The girl sat very still.

"One minute, please."

Jessica and Declan followed the bouncer leaving the girl alone.

The room gave the impression of always being tidy, modern and well kept. The walls were painted matte black and silver. Jaeger was sitting behind the desk in the middle of the room. He looked about fifty years old; his grey hair had streaks of brown. There was a plate of fried chicken on the desk. The smell of chicken rose up from the plate and suddenly Jessica realised she was starving. He smiled mid-bite and sucked the oil from his fingers. He picked up his milk and took a deep sip. Declan's eyes narrowed. He realised he was clenching his teeth; he tried to relax his jaw. Jaeger sat up and reached for his cigarettes. There was a delay before he lit one. His eyes rose towards her.

"Please have a seat."

Jessica sat down first, her shirt bunching up against the leather. Jaeger licked his tongue across his bottom lip as his eyes wandered to her thigh.

Declan pulled out his notebook. His name was sewed on the front.

Francis gave her flat eyes.

"What can I do for you, Detective Denning, I believe."

"We need to ask you some questions about the murder of Mary Talbert and Rose Nunez."

Declan pushed the photos of the victims onto the desk, the man picked them up and studied each face in detail.

"Mr Jaeger do you recognise either of these women?"

"Please Detective, call me Francis, and I'm afraid I don't recognise either."

He slid the picture back over the desk to Declan. Jaeger smiled and stood up, walking around to the front of the desk. His right hand was stretched out in front of him, his iPhone in its grasp. His left hand was behind him on the desk. Declan studied him silently. For the first time in months, he felt adrenaline soar through him. He was back in the hunt.

"Well, Francis we have evidence that both women had visited here. In fact, Miss Talbert worked here during her university placement."

Declan said. The smile disappeared from his face and thick lines formed as his eyes lowered and twitched. They were all silent for a moment. Jaeger finally cleared his throat.

"Well Jessica, I do own the most popular establishment in London and I have a lot of people coming through those doors every day. I can't take note of them all."
"This woman didn't just come, and go quietly. They made some trouble, asked too many questions and it got them killed."

He glared at her, squinting his dark eyes.

"As I said Detective I *can't* really remember her."

"No, you said you hadn't seen her. I think when people lie the first time it's because they were thinking of a good story to tell."

He crossed his arms and leaned forward. The posture signalled anger. His face looked frozen.

He moved closer to Jessica. She stood up meeting his glare.

"I've answered your questions now I would like you to leave."

She smiled and winked at him, whispering as she brushed past.

"I'm going to take you down."

He grabbed the top of her arm and dig his finger deep into her skin. She tried to pull herself away but he pulled her close to him, and whispered back.

"You know it's funny. That's exactly what Mary Talbert said and we all know what happened there, don't we, Detective?"

Jessica put a puzzled look on her face.

She pulled away, this time releasing his grip on her arm and she fell forward slightly with the force. The door swung open and the man from before stood in the frame.

"Please escort the detectives out of my casino."

A blue van was parked in front of the Dowler place. The clouds had darkened over King's Close. The house was in a quiet spot in the back of the street. The place was loud. A group of kids were enjoying a game of softball against a wall. Most of them were black. Several young women were lying on their small front lawns. They were wearing those sexy, tight sundresses. Someone shouted "BOYS, IN!" Two of the kids sprinted home. She watched them until they were gone and then carried on down the cul-de-sac.

Jessica saw the house she was looking for and started towards the door.

Jessica breathed deeply on the cigarette and then flicked the butt off into the street. A graffiti artist had sprayed there tag on the front of the house.

Jessica knocked and waited. Five minutes later, the door finally opened.

His eyes were dark brown and set into his tanned skin. He had a cheeky smile, bright eyes and a thick rumple of light hair. A shade over six foot, he was lean and his rolled sleeves showed his muscular arms.

He wore an untucked chequered shirt that looked huge against him. He quickly used his hand to smooth the hair that had fallen over his face.

She sat on the bright blue couch with faded yellow stripes. Habit carried her to cross her legs. Inside the house, it was sweltering. An old-looking Staffie wadded over to her. Jessica reached down and scratched behind its ears. The dog rolled on its back in appreciation.

Joe sat opposite bending up his knees. Jessica examined his features. He had a chilled handsome look with medium length and slightly curled hair.

"So, Mr Dowler, do you live here alone?"

There was a brief pause. Jessica was distracted for a brief moment when she caught a reflection of herself in the window. She was looking old. It angered her. The glass was covered in grime and stained from the weather. She tried to concentrate on Dowler.

"No, it's me and my sister and Tia."

He reached down to pet the dog. Jessica looked around the room for the first time. The two-bed town house was very much like a showroom. Just the necessities. A sofa, a kitchen and a few articles of clothing hung inside the door. The walls were stained where rain water had leaked in. Her mouth tightened momentarily.

"Is your sister home right now?"

"No."

"Any idea when she'll be back?"

Joe kept his eyes on her. He looked at her from under his thick brows. He looked as though he plucked them.

"She doesn't tend to follow any schedule."

Jessica laughed. Jessica liked being with men who made her feel safe. It was probably her daddy issues showing themselves.

"I have to ask some questions about your arrest seven years ago."

Joe felt a brief stirring in his gut. Their eyes locked and she saw fear quickly fill them. He gave a shame-forced smile. Jessica watched his face turn dark.

"Okay. Go ahead."

"So what happened?"

"I was arrested on suspicion of GBH but I was released because of insufficient evidence or something."

"After you were realised the Fallen Angel killed Howard Jaeger during an attack on you and your sister."

Then Jessica realised it wasn't terror in his eyes. It was anger. A long silence filled the room while Dowler thought about it. He was looking at her with captured attention. Jessica flashed him a pitying look.

"That's right. I worked for Jaeger. He was the man who testified against me."

He looked so vulnerable.

"So what happened next?"

"I don't remember anything. They drugged me."

Joe looked at her as though to confirm the memory. Jessica didn't know what to say. Jessica stopped. She tried to imagine the scene, how it must have hurt to hear his sister's screams.

"She was different after that, Ava."

"How?"

Jessica scribbled down some notes as he spoke.
Joe's smile fled and Jessica swore she felt a cold breeze on her neck.

"She's angrier than she ever was."

As they finished speaking, Ava appeared in a low cut blouse, round glasses and pinned back hair showing her smoking body. Jessica noticed a large pin above her top butt with a green stone set in it. It perfectly matched her eyes. Her hair caught the sun.

Jessica felt numb. She already wanted another cigarette.

"Ava, this is Detective Denning."

Ava looked at Jessica. Fear swelled in her eyes.

"What's going on?"

She came over and perched on the end of the sofa where Joe sat.

"She's just asking some questions about my arrest and the Fallen Angel."

At the mention of her vigilante pseudonym, her face dropped and she became more nervous.

"Oh."

"Ava, Joe was telling me you had dealing with Howard Jaeger."

She covered her face with her hands.

"It hardly seems important."

She mumbled through her fingers. She reached for Joe's hand and squeezed it.

"Why don't you tell me what this is about?"

Ava's voice sounded far away. Her eyes studied Jessica.

"I'm investigating the Angel and your case was their first reported kill."

"They killed him, that's a good thing."

"You don't believe in justice?"

"Something like that."

She blurted it out sounding guilty to her own ears. Jessica's jaw dropped open at this sign of indecisiveness.

Ava looked to her brother. Joe put a calming hand on his sister's knee. Ava's eyes slithered around the room, coming to rest on Jessica. She smiled, her blue eyes sparkling with mischief.

"Fair enough but I think you're overreacting."

Ava looked at Jessica with utter disgust.

"Well none of you lot ever fucking helped us did you."

"It's not justice to kill."

"Trust me, I know that but sometimes they don't give you a choice."

Jessica was woken by loud knocks at the door. She opened her eyes but regretted it; the lights burned. She rubbed away the white spot from her eyes and rolled over and looked at the time on her phone. It was eleven. Shit, she was late for work. She jumped up and grabbed her clothes from the day before. She changed quickly and ran downstairs. She rubbed her eyes and drank down the rest of a cold coffee from the night before. She swung open the door and ran into Declan. He jumped back and almost dropped the two cups of Starbucks in his hands.

"Jesus Jess, you look like crap."

"Thanks, what are you doing here?"

He laughed and handed her one of the cups. She sipped it down. Not caring it was scolding hot.

"You're never late so I knew something was up."

He leaned forward and could smell the alcohol on her breath.

"Late night?"

"Not really, just slept in."

"You ready for work."

She looked at her reflection in the window. She looked like crap. Declan was right. The eccentric woman that lived below stared at her. She shook her head and walked off. Probably nothing important. She scraped her hair back and tied it in a messy bun.

"Yeah, let's go."

She got in her car and drank her coffee. He looked across and opened his window. The noise from the traffic drummed in her head.

"What happened last night?"

She rubbed her head and leaned against the window. She flashed back to the years after her brother's death. The late and drunken nights. She sipped up. Drowning her feelings never worked but it dulled it.

"I just had a few drinks."

"More than a few by the look of things."

She looked across at him. But didn't change her expression.

"Can we just drop it?"

"Sure."

She had dark circles framing her eyes.

"You look, tired, Jess."

He willed his legs forward and stood in front of her desk.

"I found something about, Mary."

Jessica drank down the rest of her coffee and rubbed her eyes to stay awake.

"Go on."

"An anonymous witness said on the night Mary was killed, Francis Jaeger was frantic and angry saying Mary had stolen something from him."

"Do we know what she stole?"

"No. Francis wouldn't tell anyone, but he did say she would pay for her theft."

Jessica sat in Mary Talbert's said family kitchen. Mr and Mrs Talbert sat opposite on the breakfast bar.

"Do you have something, Detective Denning?"

The woman smiled and sipped her Earl Grey.

"We have discovered that the night Mary was killed she lost her job."

"I didn't know that, but I suppose she never really wanted to work there, she always dreamt of becoming a journalist."

"What I can't understand is he was solo paying off her student fees and yet she left her job."

"She did need the money and at first she really enjoyed working at the casino and she got well with most members of staff but towards the end she started to become distant, when we asked about it. The university arranged an internship with the local paper and then on that day she came to see us in the morning filled with excitement about a story she had that would guarantee her a permanent job with the paper."

Mrs Talbert began crying softly.

"Excuse me."

She walked into the living room and shut the door to mask the sound of her sobbing. The husband turned back and smiled at the detectives.

"If I'm honest with you, Mary didn't really tell us about these things. She was always afraid we would worry. She told her friend Melanie everything. You'd be better asking her."

Jessica drove back to the station, her black car halted in the steady traffic. She felt a sharp pain run up her side. She ran her hand down under her belt and rubbed her hip. She dialled Declan's number on her car phone. While she waited, she dug into the Oder pocket pulling out the small sheet of Paracetamol. She took two with the rest of her bottle of water and threw it on the back seat. Finally, Declan picked up.

"Hello."

"I need you to find Melony Pirelli. She was the victims best friend her parents sad she would most likely know more."

"She's here."

"What do you mean?"

"Melonie she's waiting at your desk."

She ran her hand down her side again as the pain started to ease.

"I'll be there in an hour. Traffic's hell."

She hung up and looked out the window. A motorbike sped past catching the light between each building.

She pulled into her space outside Scotland Yard and ran up the stairs to her desk. Jessica sat down in her chair in front of Melanie. The young woman looked up at her with bloodshot eyes. She had a cut running down the length of her sharp cheek.

"Miss Pirelli. How can I help you?"

"I'm here about Mary Talbert. I know who killed her and they're trying to kill me."

All day, Melony had been twitchy. She felt eyes on her in the interrogation room. Jessica always felt that she should be better prepared—forewarned, ready. That sort of thing. So when turned up at the station talking about her case, she felt a failure. Her cheekbones were hidden under plumpness, her eyes were sunken into her skin and the untidily cut fringe was swept across her forehead. The years had not been kind to Melony. But her skin was still olive coloured.

Melony's shoulders were hunched defensively around her chest.

"Who is trying to kill you?"

"Francis-fucking-Jaeger."

Her voice came out cramped and hoarse. Though she had tried to make it fill the room.

"How do you mean he tried to kill you?"

"Don't fuck with me, Detective."

She smacked a pack of cigarettes on her palm.

"You mind?"

She asked as she opened it. Jessica held her hands up. Melanie went on.

"It's my own fault you know, I fall in love with the wrong people."

She leaned back into the chair and smoked the cigarette.

"What happened, Melony?"

"Mary got an internship with the Stanwood Times, she had always dreamed of being a journalist."

Jessica thought about it. The Stanwood Times were the most popular local newspaper – it made sense. Melony paused and looked around, taking another drag on her cigarette.

"We spent a drunken night together. A mistake. But it wasn't that for me; she knew I loved her."

Jessica's throat closed in pity.

"Was that the last you saw her?"

"Not quite. She came to me a few weeks ago really excited about this story she had heard on her shift at the casino. I tried to warn her but she wouldn't listen, she kept following the story."

She put her cigarette out on the table.

"She must have told you something to warrant this attack."

"She had heard about this book that he kept which had every dirty secret inside it and she was going to steal. She told me she was going to blow it all wide open in her first article."

"What happened?"

"She came to me before her shift the day before she was killed. She overheard an argument she was so upset. She said she was going to do her shift and then she was getting out."

"So what went wrong?"

"I saw her the night she was killed, you know. She came to give me the book she stole. I was so angry with her that I just slammed the door on her face."

"What happened to the book?"

"I threw it away. I know it was wrong but I was scared."

"What did you tell Jaeger, Melony?"

"I told them everything I knew. But I didn't tell them I had gone back for the book but it wasn't there."

Jessica thought of the ledger. She wondered how many crimes were detailed in it.
Melanie interrupted her thoughts.

"She was sorry. Last thing she said to me and I let her die."

Jessica nodded and said nothing but didn't look away.

"I promise I will keep you safe."

Melany smiled and Jessica thought she could see disbelief in her eyes. She stood and walked over to the door. Jessica hesitated before saying.

"One more thing, what argument did Mary over hear?"

"Francis Jaeger was asking about the murder of a prostitute or some shit."

Jessica's eyes grew wide. A strong smile spread across her face.

Jessica dragged deeply on a cigarette and dropped the butt into a drain. Declan stared out across the green landscape the crowds of people were hurtling through.

She started walking across the street to the square patch of grass that lined the front of the media buildings. She could see the bodies of homeless men and women, sprawled asleep on the grass.

They looked like bodies left after a war. The place was crowded with people and covered in a veil of cigarette smoke. They had all come to wait out the traffic but either got too comfortable or wasted.

Jessica went down to the end of the grass where the benches were empty and stood opposite one of the homeless men.

She looked down at the short, dark man with a full brown beard split like curtains. He wore khaki jeans and two pulled over jumpers. The man looked around until their eyes met and Jessica nodded once.

The man pulled a sleeping bag up around his neck. The lights on the street cut out and until Jessica's eyes adjusted it felt like they were dropping through the darkness. Finally, she felt her foot impact on the grass and let her body relax slightly. A foul odour greeted Jessica as she bent down. She recognised it as the smell of a drunk's breath. There were empty bottles on nearly every inch of the grass. The man's space was very much like the owner. It showed a dismal life; if it be called a life at all.

She looked at the body next to him. It was a woman. Not very attractive. Except to the man. There were tattooed lines dripping down her cheek from her right eye.

"Mr Wilson?"

About thirty feet away, there were half-a-dozen Latino workers loading boxes onto trollies. Jessica noted that each of the boxes was just about the size of a small table. The boxes were being moved to a white van with a forklift. The driver's side door was open and a white man sat watching the workers. Another white man was leaning against the van studying a clipboard. 'System Hygiene,' was printed on the side of the van in pale blue letters. The hordes of homeless men and woman ran to the van and grabbed the scraps the workers dropped.

"They are lucky. Its delivery day."

There was a note of triumph in the man's voice.

Jessica took the morgue photo of Rose Nunez out of her pocket and slid it across the ground. The man didn't touch the photo but he looked down at it. He showed no reaction to it. He used the end of his thumb to press his glasses up on the bridge of his nose.

"Jessica Denning, Scotland Yard."

"I figured you were a cop. What can I do for you?"

"Where were you sleeping Thursday night?"

"Near the bins by a fancy block of flats."

He smiled and showed Jessica his decaying teeth.

"Did you recognise the woman?"

The man jerked his head back and poured down half a bottle of beer. The man's stench had filled the air. Jessica held her coat up to her mouth and nose so she would smell perfume instead of the homeless man.

"No, never seen her."

Jessica acted as though she hadn't heard much of what he was saying before and took notes.

"Did you see anything Thursday night?"

"I saw a woman putting something in the bins where we was sleeping."

Jessica was getting the idea he was just someone who watched.

His voice trailed off and he just stared at the tucks.

"Did you see what she put in the bin?"

"Shit that nobody wants. Books and stuff. The girl was upset though. Never seen anyone looking scared like that. Screwed me up, man."

"Then what happened?"

"She saw me behind one of the bins and she ran off."

"Why did she run?"

Jessica was wearing out her welcome.

"I tend to scare people; running isn't the worst thing to happen."

Jessica thought of Joe. She was sure he was wrong.
Jessica was thinking quickly. What else was there to ask?

"What about the book? That's the part that doesn't fit. What happened to it?"

The man looked down at the woman next to him and avoided Jessica's eye contact. His hazel eyes widened with fear.

"I took it. There were some photos and shit as well. Just thought I'll flog it for a tenner."

"Who did you sell it to?"

"A fucking nonce. He came to buy it and kept watching Ava. Thinking abou…"

He trailed off his words.

"He started touching her so I started on him but I was wired off my tits; couldn't fucking move."

Tears spilled from his eyes and he began to moan low, as if there was a terrible pain inside him.
Jessica thought for a moment.

"Did he give you a name?"

"Yeah, took some fucking doing mind but I got it. Outsmarted the bastard."

"What name did he give you?"

"Joe Dowler."

"Are you sure it was Joe Dowler?"

"Yes ma'am. Ain't never gonna forget that man. That's why we come here, safer you know."

They moved on to small talk for a moment and then said goodbye. Talking to the man sealed it. She rubbed her hand across the small tattoo below her ear. She ran her hand among the small butterfly outline. She got it when her brother died and it always comforted her to feel it there.

It was three-thirty by the time Jessica pulled up outside the home where Joe Dowler lived. The lights were still on but the curtains were drawn and there were cars on the driveway. After Declan hung up, Jessica pocketed her phone, and lit a cigarette at the window.

Jessica pocketed her cigarettes and got out of the car. She had to knock twice, and when the door opened it was Joe Dowler himself. He opened it just as wide as his own body. Jessica noticed that this sleeves were tight on his biceps.

"What can I do for you?"

His optimism mirrored Declan.

Jessica looked around on the doorstep, before turning back to Joe and answering.

"Can we talk inside?"

He opened up and led him into the room, and to the couch where she sat last time. Jessica and Declan sat down; Jessica began making there introductions.

"Mr Dowler…"

"You can call me Joe."

"Joe then, we are investigating the murder of Rose Nunez."

"A homeless man has come forward and claimed he sold you a ledger."

"And you believe him."

"He had another way to know you."

"Maybe I did if I saw this guy selling something."

"So did you buy it?"

"I don't remember but I could have, yeah."

"Did you know it was stolen from Francis Jaeger?"

"I wouldn't buy it not if it was about him."

"Joe, my witness says you gave your name."

"If I was trying to hide it, that would be a fucking stupid move."

His fear turned to anger and his hand stopped trembling. Joe put his fists on the table and went forward. He didn't have to lean far. His height helped make his point. He shook his head and managed a smile. There was no joy in it.

He swung back in his chair and rubbed his hand through his light hair.

Declan leaned to Jessica's ear and whispered,

"Wilson sent a drawing of who he saw."

He passed his phone over to Jessica. He leaned in close to the screen and studied the face. It wasn't Joe Dowler. The man in the photo had much harsher features and a darker face. She passed the phone over to Joe.

"Do you recognise who this is?"

Joe leaned forward and started couching into his hand. His body jerked forward. He looked at the photo for a long moment before speaking,

"That's my dad."

Sweat was falling down out of his hair and drying in the cool air on his neck. Joe looked down at the phone in his hands and then slowly passed it back. There may have been pity in his eyes, but mostly disgust.

"I'm sorry, Joe."

That was all she could think to say. He shook his head as if to shake off her sympathy.

"When did you last see him?"

"Twenty-one fucking years. He did horrible things," he said.
"Evil things, and I still can't tell you."

He was acting calm but he wasn't. They talked about his father for nearly an hour. Jessica and Declan mostly listened. But all she could do was once more offer him sympathy.

Jessica was disgusted with herself. Solving cases was about getting people to talk to you; not forcing them to talk. She had forgotten that this time.

Ava began hunting down her father. She walked down an alley and to a black door at the back. She knocked three times before it opened.

"What's the club's name?"

A pair of dark eyes stared through the gap in the door.

"The Deviant."

The door fully opened flooding the alley with deep red light. She walked through the crowded club. The circular stage was surrounded by drooling men. Each one turned their head as Ava approached the bar and sat on the last red bar stool and summoned the bartender over. An older woman approached. She bent over the bar giving a clear eye down her waistcoat. Ava could see the deep scars that ran under the curves of her breasts. The skin was pale and blotchy.

"What can I do for you, honey, you here to audition?"

Her voice was aged more than her body.

"I'm here to ask you about this man."

She slammed the picture of her father on the bar. The woman slipped her hand under the bar and flicked a small switch beneath. She slipped the picture back across the bar. Her smile replaced with a stern and slanted lip.

"Don't know him. A lot of men come through here, love, can't remember them all."

Ava chewed down on her gum and pushed the picture back to the woman.

"I think you'd remember him, Miss."

She smiled showing her dazzling teeth. The woman became uncomfortable and shuffled on her feet.

"You're right I do know him, but you know what stupid bitch, I'm not telling you anything."

With her words something inside Ava snapped. She grabbed a handful of bleached hair and slammed her head down on the bar. The woman's nose bled heavily over the image. She tried to lift her head but Ava slammed it back down.

"Try again, Miss. He's Simon Dowler, now where can I find him?"

The woman struggled but stayed reluctant in her silence. Ava pulled her back up by her hair and slammed her head down on the bar a second time. She skid the side of her face on a broken glass and bled, covering the bar. No one moved; there were too entranced to tear away from the dancers who just kept going in the hope they would get a tip.

"Okay he comes here every week and he lives in the hotel at the Blackened Hill Casino."

Two men stormed through the club approaching the bar. She lifted her head blood still streaming down her face and grimaced as she pulled a shard of glass from the wound. They looked around but Ava had disappeared somewhere into the crowd of depraved men. The woman spat a small pile of blood on the bar and rubbed the moisture from her lips.

Ava stood by the back door and breathed heavily against the wall. The rain beat hard on her skin as she walked through the lit streets to the casino. The casino stood luminous against the black sky. The green LEDs shadowed onto the pavement summoning its victims through the glass doors. She walked up to the front desk and pulled her hood high over her face. The woman at the desk smiled. She was wearing a Hawaiian skirt and a coconut bra.

"Aloha! How much would you like changed for you today?"

"What room is Simon Dowler in?"

The woman stopped smiling and signalled over to two men. They walked over and stood directly behind Ava breathing heavily with each step.

"I'm afraid I can't tell you, it's confidential."

Ava stopped chewing her gum and pulled her hand into a fist without realising the strength of her grip digging into her palm.

"I'm his hired entertainment."

She lowered her hood pulling it down around her neck and ran her hands through her long hair making it slightly as she combed through. The woman studied her face and embraced the beauty and picked up the phone off her desk. Her eyes continued to track Ava's curves. She chewed her gold nail in the side of her mouth.

"Your new miss… what was your name, girl?"

"Just tell him she's from Dream Desires."

The phone clicked as it answered.

"Sir I have a woman from Dream Desires."

She nodded her head and wrote on the page behind the desk. While she spoke, her voice turned deep and full of desire. She slammed the phone down on the desk and nodded at Ava.

"He says go on up, he's in Room 105."

The two men walked back into the busy casino floor.

Ava walked up the brown stairs and studied each floor sign. Finally, she reached the door on the fifth floor and walked down the long corridor, until she came to Room 105 and knocked hard. The door shook against its hinge. The number '1' flipped upside down on its nail. The door swung open and cast a strip of shadow across the corridor. A large man stood in the entrance wearing a pair of striped blue boxers, his protruding stomach hanging over covered in patches of wire-thin grey hairs.

"Come on in then, girl."

Ava chewed her gum frantically the rage building inside. She walked into the room taking in the plain décor and unclean walls. The man walked close behind her his stomach pressing into her back and lay down on the bed. Ava slipped off her coat and placed it on the back of the brown chair and put down her dark bag on the desk and pulled out a roll of thick twine. The man studied her as she twisted the rope between her fingers. Her knuckles turned a pale white with the strength of her grip. She dropped the rope back down onto the desk and pulled out the long carved knife from the bag.

"What the hell are you doing, girl?"

She turned holding a knife in her right hand and smiled a twisted, manic smile. Her pupils had fully dilated taking out all the colour and kindness from her eyes. She lurched forward into the thin isle next to the bed. Simon sprang onto his feet and pushed forward against Ava. She grabbed his arm pulling it with such force she yanked the joint from its socket. He fell back onto the bed gripping the already swollen flesh. He felt the cavity where his skin had fallen in and screamed out. Ava pulled the arm back and shackled him to the top of the cheap wooden headboard. She brought the rope over and dropped it onto the brown throw which was sprawled across the bed. The metal of the cuff instantly carved into the weak wood. She felt the shoulder dislocation bringing her knee up and onto the blade. She thrust down with intense pressure. The shoulder snapping back into place. Simon screeched in agony. His eyes wide with pain and fear. She stroked along the rough throat until her hands met with the twine rope. She brought it to the top of his leg and tied it tight around his exposed thigh. She pulled the knot until the skin turned white as the blood was forced away from the area. She walked back over to the mirror and watched herself in the mirror for a moment. Her eyes grew wide and filled with colour. A thin line of salty tears formed. She tightly shut her eyes forcing back the pain and grabbed the carved blade from the desk. She turned back to Simon and flipped the knife playfully in her hands. He stared up at her with the same silvery blue eyes she had. She pulled her arm back and stabbed the blade into the fat of his thigh. As it pierced the skin, a thick flow of blood pushed against the blade. The man gazed at her his eyes were filled with pain. She twisted the knife and tore open the skin and pulled out the blade, the steel catching on the ledge of torn flesh. The gash was so deep she could see the yellow tissue of fat clinging to his muscles. As she stroked up his thigh her fingertips glided in the blood. She grabbed the knot and pulled the rope from his bleeding thigh. Blood flowed back to the open wound, blood spilling from the deep gash. He breathed heavily through the pain, his chest heaving for air. His lips parted and began turning purple as the oxygen was stolen from his lungs.

"What do you want?"

She smiled pushing the gum to the side of her mouth and breathing in heavily.

"Where's the ledger?"

He smirked. His yellowed teeth clung limply to his pale gums.

"Damned if I'm telling you, girl."

He pulled his chest in pushing his saliva up from his stomach and spitting it at Ava.

She pulled back and wiped it off with the cuff of her sleeve and walked over to the desk picking up the gun. She slid back and loaded the barrel, listening as the bullet clicked into place. She aimed it at his head and then lowering it to his knee. Her eyes squinted as she concentrated on the target. She twitched her finger against the trigger planting a bullet deep in his kneecap. Blood sprayed over the back walls and over the hideous bedspread.

She walked back over chewing her gum at a more controlled pace, enjoying the thrill of the game and placed her hand on the bullet hole feeling how it shot straight through the bone. Ava pushed her finger into the gash feeling as the bone scratched against the leather of her glove. Feeling deep for the small compressed bullet and fingered it out. Blood gushed from the new wound. He coughed; blood stained his teeth and leaked down onto his chin. He pushed his tongue to the front of his mouth and wiped it across his lips.

"Okay please it's in the safe, just stop this."

She stared down at him as he lifted his bloated arm and pointed across the plywood desk in the corner. She went over to the sparsely concealed safe hidden between cheap slats of the desk, she shot the lock opening it with ease. She pulled back the heavy steel door. The door ground open in an already worn track. Flecks of dust and wood flew out onto the carpet.

She looked through it finding nothing but disturbed images of different companions in compromising positions. She felt the bottom-lined with wine-red felt.—it seemed strange though hollow. She stroked across the edges feeling a slight lip in the felt. She pulled it up slowly revealing a small silver handle. She unclasped it pulling the heavy steel that fought to keep the secrets kept hat way. She pulled out the thick long leather-bound book, Blackened Hill Casino carved in loop-golden lettering across the front. The smell of old pages and leather filled the space. She flicked through the pages loaded with names, dates and actions.

She placed it carefully in a cloth bag putting it inside a lined shoulder bag. She picked up her knife walking over to their father placing the cold steel blade against his thick neck; he gulped pushing his flesh against the blade slitting it slightly. A small drop of blood ran down into the dragon engraving of the side.

"Do you know who I am?"

He looked deep in her eyes examining the features of her face, noting all her attributes—he figured it out. He smiled, laughing slightly in a sick controlling way. He leaned his head back against the headboard.

"Mary Dowler. You look just like her now."

The mention of her mother's name brought tears lining her bottom eyelid. He moved his neck back against the blade as memories came flooding back to Ava.

"Why did you leave?"

He pushed against the blade and her grip on it lessened dropping it to the floor, a slight thud as it hit. He laughed cynically and coughed through the pain. He brought his hand up to rest on his swollen shoulder.

"I got what I wanted from your mother when she finally told me she had given birth to twins. I had someone kill her. I searched for you to truly cover it all up but I couldn't. Now look at you, more like me than you care to admit, except you look the spitting image of 'Virgin Mary,' oh so innocent, till me of course."

She picked the knife off the soaked floor and placed it back against his neck nicking into the pre-made scrape. He leaned back and closed his eyes and gripped hard on his muscle. Ava pulled the knife away, despite all he had done, she couldn't kill him. She turned to leave picking up the gun from the end of the brown bed and replied to what he had called her mother 'Virgin Mary.' The rage inside her rekindled and she swung the gun back, pointing it directly between his eyes. The bullet travelled through the air silently until it struck through his skull and lodged in his brain killing him instantly. She looked at her father laying half-naked covered in blood. The tears fell at a rapid pace and stained her cheeks.

Jessica stood in front of the crime scene tape and ducked below it. She studied the numbers on each door and walked down the long corridor. The note in her hand told her she was looking for suite 105. She stopped when she saw the door. The cheap wood was peeling off the hinges. She gagged when she walked through the door. The walls were stained with blood and the smell was rancid. The corpse was shackled to the bed by his wrists. They had been broken and twisted into an angular position.

Jessica stood there stunned. He had one of those fleshy, red faces that fat cats like him always seemed to have. The scars on his face seemed to darken as she watched. She felt on the verge of tears. She stopped at the foot of the bed and gathered herself.

She thought of the pain and horror Ava inflicted for justice. She knew they deserved it. But justice always came at a cost for those who deliver it. The thought turned her stomach.

"It's them, you know. The Fallen Angel."

Hearing the name made her grimace.

"I know."

Jessica recognised the man. It was Simon Dowler. She could see Ava in his piercing blue eyes. She put a little steel in her voice.

"Have we found the ledger?"

Declan shook his head and gestured towards the desk.

"They think it must have been in there."

She walked over to the desk and crouched down. The safe was empty. It was then, staring at the felt lining, that she noticed something odd. The bottom was slanted and raised. She slid her hand in the hidden cavity. Nothing, she stood up.

"It's gone. What about cause of death?"

Watts folded his hands and put them on the desk.

"Bullet to the head."

"Can you say for sure it's the Angel?"

Watts looked at the coroner and nodded.

"Yes, we are certain."

She started to turn in order to leave and check the body again. But before she could she felt a sharp buzz against her thigh. She fished in her pocket for the phone and answered it.

"Hello?"

"Detective Denning,"

"Yes, sir."

She knew the voice. It was the Chief.

"We've had another call. I want you to follow Watts and the coroner to the scene."

"Yes, sir."

She hung up and rested her hand on her head. Pain began burning behind her eyes. She checked her watch. It was noon. Her chest tightened as if there was no air left in the room.

Declan followed Jessica along the road to the abandoned building at the end. Watts walked a few paces ahead of them. He always wanted to be the first on the scene. When he saw the open door he skipped through it.

The streets seemed deserted when they arrived. There were no patrol cars and where the press usually stood, buzzing for a story, empty.

The body was strung up from heating pipe on the ceiling. Stanley Watts stood examining the deep gash across his back. His hair was swept across a bald patch on the back of his head and his collar was stained with sweat.

"We found a wallet in his trouser pocket."

Watts said. He threw the small evidence bag to Declan. He caught it with one hand and passed it across. Jessica flipped it open and read the ID card in the clear card slip.

"Mr Fromisire."

She didn't know the name.

"Head of King's College, where I went."

Watts childishly struck his breast after he spoke.

"Did you find anything else on him?"

He walked over and stood in front of Jessica. He smelt strongly of industrial disinfectant and cheap cologne. He handed her a folded note, covered in dried blood.

"We found this lodged in one of his wounds."

Jessica read the cursive writing of the Angel's note and rubbed her head again. Watts read it over her shoulder and ran his hand through his thin hair again. The pain began to burn down her neck. She wrote everything down on the pocketbook she carried.

"The other body is the same."

Jessica and Declan looked up. Watts' grey moustache was yellow with tobacco and wriggled as he spoke. Declan always thought he looked old and worn.

"The other body."

He nodded and pointed across the floor to a stream of dried blood which ran from a hollowed body. She walked over. Her heels stuck in the blood. The body was drained and sunken. The flesh was being torn towards the floor by gravity.

"Do we know who the victim is?"

Watts stood behind her so his shoulder pressed against her arm. She could hear her strained breath.

"It's hard to recognise him. His face is pretty bad. We know he was killed by having all the blood drained from his body."

He shuddered slightly as he imagined the victim's death. Jessica looked at the man's face. His skin had caved in around his skull and his eyes bulged out from his head. The colour had drained and left only the darkness of each pupil.

"How long will it be till we get dental ID?"

"I never said I couldn't tell that it was. Lucky for you I found his badge near the body."

"Badge?"

"This is Deputy Chief Constable Harry Clayton."

"Shit!"

Declan cursed under his breath.

She hated the taste of the poisoned words that were about to spew from her mouth.

"I have a suspicion of who it is."

Declan looked across at her with tired eyes. His eyebrows pulled close together and his head tilted to the side. He mirrored her posture and leaned forward.

"Who?"

"Ava Dowler."

He saw what he could have seen all along. Adrenaline rushed into his veins and sent his blood running as it all came together.

"Really? Christ! I'll have uniforms pick her up."

"No she doesn't know we suspect her. I'll bring her in quietly."

"Not on your own, Jess."

"I'll be fine. Stay and wrap things up for me. And keep Watts away from any press."

He smiled and walked over to the other body. Jessica got back in her car and dry-swallowed two Paracetamols. The headache burning behind her eyes.

Ava rubbed her damp eyes and blinked hard. She hustled down the hallway, and down the stairs to the living room.

What will he say? Ava thought about it. But she didn't know the answer. She debated whether it was the right time. She had to knock twice before Joe opened the door. She had been crying. For a moment Joe said nothing.

"What's going on, Ava?"

"Joe I have something I need to tell you."

Even as she said it, there was hesitation in her voice. His voice was a whisper and calmed her. He flashed her a smile so like hers it stabbed her every time.

"Go on then."

"There are things I've done. Pain that I've caused."

Joe spread his hands and stepped closer to Ava. She smoothly raised her hand to stop him. She realised how hard it was to admit.

"I killed those people."

She pointed at the open newspaper on the table. Joe followed her eyes down.

"What do you mean?"

"You know what I mean. You know what they call me."

She took a step closer to him. But he moved back. He started to cry. It was unbearable. He looked hurt. She found the silence in the room difficult. He just shook his head.

"You mean the Fallen Angel. There's no way."

She didn't need to say anymore so she just nodded.

Ava closed her eyes and felt her world cave in around her. Silence. For a moment she thought she had lost him. He crossed the room and hugged her deep and hard. The faint smell of vanilla wafted up. That was all she needed. She tensed at his touch. He tightly shut his eyes and held his breath. That was always how he hugged. It made Ava smile but the pain in her face. It never left.

"I'm so sorry, Joe. I'm sorry for being selfish."

He sighed loudly and met her eye. He was crying. She had never seen him sob like this. She nodded into his shirt.

"You're not selfish, Ava, you're in pain."

Jessica flicked through the pages of the ledger. Her finger cut against the thin edge of the page and leaving a small spot of blood on the edge. She sucked the end of her finger filling her mouth with the metallic taste of blood. She felt on the last page of the book an envelope. She pulled out the pictures and flipped through them and dropped them down onto her desk. Declan pushed open the interrogation room door and gestured across at Jessica.

"Jess, are you going to question Mrs Harvey?"

She stood up and grabbed the ledger and the images off her desk and walked over to Declan. She pushed through the door and rested against the back wall. Her heel rested in the groove between the bricks. Mrs Harvey sat at the table in the centre of the room. She was clean cut and smiling. A smirk spread across her face and the room filled with her arrogance. Her lips were stained with yellow tar.

"Mrs Harvey, we have evidence that you killed and tortured the young woman who worked and lived at the youth hostel near where you worked."

She laughed slightly a smile creeping across her aged face. She glared across at Jessica her eyes blazing with anger as they wandered over her figure.

"Detective Denning, I'm a very a busy woman and you can't touch me."

She stood to leave picking up her expensive red leather bag and turned to head for the door. Jessica stood and placed down each incriminating image they had of her, spreading them across the desk.

"Sit down, Mrs Harvey."

The woman turned back, her phone pressed against her ear, she saw the pictures. The phone fell from her hand as the shock entrapped her. She sat down and picked up the nearest photograph. She examined it realising she had been caught and there was no way out.

"I'll make a deal if I get to walk out of here. I'll tell you everything about the Blackened Hill Casino."

Jessica nodded in agreement to her deal.

"Francis Jaeger approached me five years ago telling me he knew my desires; he knew the anger I felt at all these young women with their life ahead of them living and working in a hostel, everything coming to them with such ease, the beauty of their world radiating on their pretty and un-aged faces. Francis told me he understood and explained his desire to be a god watching over, ensuring every one of his mortals explored their deepest fantasies. He told me he had one of these mortals who worked at the hostel they provided the girls, and I made them pay for their beauty. In return, I covered up another mortal's desire sending sixth form children who never came back. I just choose children with no attachments so no one would care if they lived or died or whatever they had planned."

Jessica wrote down every detail; all the strands and dots slowly connecting, painting the final picture.

"What do you know about Francis Jaeger?"

"He thinks he's a god above everyone, he liked to be called Lucifer—god of chaos—who was thrown from heaven for creating a war. He found you and comforted you. He let you explore your desires and in return cover up others."

"Did he ever tell you who he was making you cover for?"

She clasped her hands and rested them on the edge of the table. Tapping her red nails against the steel. The skin on her neck hung loose against her coat.

"No, but it wasn't hard to figure out, I was always told to feed the child a lie, sending them to the Mayor's office either for work experience or because the Mayor needed to talk to them."

Jessica had a confession, a testimony, against both Francis Jaeger and the honourable Mayor. She stood collecting the images. This time, as she turned to leave, Vera stopped her jumping to her knees and grabbing Jessica's arm. Jessica flinched as she rubbed the bruises from her meeting with Francis Jaeger.

"I can leave now then, you remember our deal."

Jessica pushed her back down onto the chair and bent over the desk, her face coming close to Vera's. She pushed the desk into Vera's legs.

"I lied."

"Detective I can use that against you, think this through."

"Mrs Harvey when the people hear of your disgusting crimes against innocent girls, they will stick a badge on my chest. Good luck in prison, Vera."

Without saying another word, Jessica walked towards the door. She left slamming the door behind and preparing herself of her next round of questioning. She walked down the corridor to the interrogation room. The headache still burned like a fire inside her head.

Jessica opened the door of the next room. Dan Declan followed in close behind her, crossing his muscular arms across his chest and glared at the man sitting opposite.

The man sitting across from them was fat, late fifties with red and unhealthy skin. He wore a tight suit which clung to his fat body. The top button was undone and a long tie hung loosely around his wide neck and his stomach pushed through the gap between each button. He watched Declan closely. His face turned bright red and angry while he crossed his legs.

"Mr Patrick Johnston, I have evidence of horrendous crimes you committed."

Declan said. He placed the file on the desk and spread the images in front of Patrick.

He pulled himself forward his red plump fingers grasping the image next to his stomach. He studied the boy in the image, his lips turning up slightly in a crooked smile. He flipped the image back across the desk towards Declan. He looked down and shook his head.

"You kidnapped and tortured these boys, keeping them prisoner putting them through all manner of hell, then Francis Jaeger would take them off your hands and dispose of each body."

Declan stood and pressed his gripped fist into the desk.

"I want a deal, I'll tell you everything I have on Lucifer and in return I get to go free."

"I'm afraid you're not calling the shots anymore, Mr Johnston, we are, and here's what's going to happen. You're going to tell us what you know and in return well ask the DA to put you in a secluded cell otherwise you'll go in with the rest and they don't usually take kindly to people like you. They will torture you just as you tortured those boys."

The sweat dripped off Patrick's forehead and caught on his thick eyebrows. He pushed his finger in his collar and released his tie. Ketchup stains ran down his neck. He thought about it for a moment until he sighed and spoke.

"I'll take the deal. Lucifer—Francis Jaeger, approached me one day, I couldn't help but tell everything to him. How much I hated hiding my want to hurt and destroy. He told me with his help, I wouldn't have to anymore and in return all I'd have to do was use my position as an MP to cover up and rig what I was told. It was too good to pass up. I thought he was crazy, talking of how he was a god among scared mortals terrified of the human nature to kill, but he gave me what I wanted. He sent the boys to me and hid my indiscretions. He told us he wouldn't keep anything that could tie the crimes to us but I figured he had lied. He wanted power and so I knew he had kept something but I got what I wanted and so did he."

The detectives left the room leaving Patrick Johnston alone in the room with the thoughts of his past and future swirling around in his head. Jessica was right–Mr Johnston felt more fear than he had ever in his life.

Just as Jessica and Declan began to question their third suspect, a uniformed officer stationed to guard the holding cell, knocked timidly on the door. His face was soaked and dripping with sweat, his skin shined when the light hit his perspiration. He coughed and spluttered as he requested Jessica to come and see him. She walked out closing the door in the corridor. She could see his face was not just wet from sweat but from tears as well. He told her that Ava Dowler had escaped from holding; he was apologetic and terrified of losing his job.

Jessica raced down the stairs to the holding cells. She approached the first one on the left. The man who had been sitting in the corner, was now laying on the floor, a crack in his head with a small circle of blood entangled in his unkempt hair. Jessica approached the man placing her index, and middle fingers on his cold neck. She stayed still listening until finally she heard a heartbeat, slow, but present. His lungs were clawing for air.

Jessica searched the cell finding a photo wedged under the leg of the metal bed. She pulled it out, the metal scraping on the concrete floor. She held it up to the dim light. It was the photo of the day Ava and Jessica had spent together; the amazing time they had had together came flooding back to the front of her memories, the light shone through the image revealing writing on the back, she flipped the image.

"Until next time, Detective."

The combination of the image, the words and her missing love became too much and a tear fell but she didn't have time for that. Her investigation was deep into the Blackened Hill Casino and she had nearly closed it.

Jessica pulled up in front of the un-lit casino. The front door stood like the opening of a cave.

They barged their way into the casino—it was empty. Tickets and paper littered the red carpets, the machines were all dark. The only light came from a crack under a door at the back of the casino and up a marbled staircase. Declan stood to the side and covered Jessica as she creaked opened the door. She felt the shock travel up her arms as the door slammed into something. Blood trickled under the ledge in the door.

"Police! Come out now! There's no escape we have the building surrounded."

She listened carefully. Straining for the slightest sound. Nothing.

"We're coming in."

She squeezed through the small gap in the doorframe. The metal handle cut against her stomach as she pushed her way through. She looked down at the slate floor and saw exactly what had stopped the door. Francis Jaeger's body lay sprawled in front of the door. Blood covered every inch of the slate floor around the body. His beak was covered in slits and bullet holes that had punctured through the skin. Jessica could tell he had fractured shoulders as the skin around his joints had caved in, a sharp shard of bone protruded from his right leg. His face had been beaten. It was bruised and red, and scratches from a woman's nails ran down his cheek. His lifeless eyes were wide and they stared up at Jessica. She felt a sharp chill run down her spine.

She saw a small pointed corner of white paper peeping out from his jacket pocket. She pulled. It was stained with drops of blood and torn slightly in a struggle. It was the Angel. She read the familiar cursive writing. Ava's soft and alluring voice narrated it within her head, "Through hell found Justice and now so will He."

Jessica felt the slight raised and still wet ink and she crouched down on her knees close to the body. Blood sticking to the bottom shoes.

Stanley Watts came up the stairs. Taking two at a time and stumbling on the last one. He knelt down beside the body and did his checks.

"Cause of death is prolonged bleeding."

"How long's he been dead?"

Watts ran his finger across the blood.

"Only a few hours."

Two men lifted the body onto the open black stretcher. Watts zipped it up and stood up close to Jessica.

"Anything else?"

"We'll have to test at the lab but if it's the Angel I wouldn't hold your breath."

Jessica walked over to the black glass desk in the middle of the room and opened the second drawer. It creaked as it stuck against the wood. She ran her finger under the ledge and felt a gap between the wood and glass.

She pushed her fingers into the gap and felt as far down as she could, before pulling hard against the desk and tore the front of the draw from the wood. A hole had been hollowed out of the thick wood lining in the drawer. Inside, she found details of every crime he had investigated; she pulled the papers, as they emptied the carved hole, a gun fell out. She picked it up, it was an expensive, carved, white-handled silver barrel, loaded with five of the six bullets. Declan picked up the gun and put it in the evidence bag. He admired the detail for a moment

"No witnesses again."

"No, I didn't think so."

He rubbed his finger along the barrel of the gun and felt the carved design.
"The Angel's going to walk."

"We know her name."

"She knows that. She's long gone by now."

"I don't blame her. These men deserved to die."

"Don't let the Chief hear you say that."

He laughed and leaned against the desk. Jessica stood and became level with him. She smiled but in a sad way and gently rubbed her tattoo.

"Let's go."

"You sure there's nothing else?"
"Yep the case is over."

She walked out the door Declan close behind her.

Jessica watched from the stage as the crowds of platoon officers filled the rows of seats. The media helicopters circled overhead. The smell of fresh-cut grass was strong in the place. She walked to the back and sat next to Declan. They looked at each other for a long moment. He nodded,
"You okay?"

Jessica nodded but didn't look up. She weeded through her pockets. But she had no cigarettes left.

"Here."

Jessica looked up at Declan. He was passing her a small pack of lambert and butler. Two thin cigarettes protruded out.

"Thanks, Declan."

He smiled and pulled out one of the cigarettes. Jessica took the last one and nodded. She reached into her pocket and pulled out a lighter. They left the stage. Outside, Jessica lit her cigarette and heavily breathed air through it. Tasting it. Savouring it. She drew the smoke fully into her lungs and held it there.

She usually only took rolled cigarettes and menthol tips. The taste of straight tobacco tasted horrible. But she was desperate for a smoke. She thumbed the lighter and put it in her pocket. She felt something else in there and pulled it out. It was the photo from the holding cell. She rubbed her thumb across it and squeezed it tightly in her hand and then put it back in her pocket.

A long black car pulled up in front of her. She looked at the blacked out windows. The doors opened on either side of the car and the new Mayor and Deputy Chief stepped out. They walked briskly to the stage and stood fifty yards away from Jessica.

"Are you ready, detectives?"

Jessica flicked her cigarette off into the park and nodded. She followed the two men back onto the stage and re-took her seat. The Chief looked at Jessica and didn't flinch in his stare. He had a knowing smile which was reassuring. He finally looked away and focused on the crowds of cameras.

"You will never find a more dedicated team of people. The Scotland Yard homicide detectives are an essential asset in crime prevention."

A roar of applause erupted through the crowds. He raised a hand and continued his speech.

"Detective Jessica Denning and her partner Detective Declan Hughes have revealed an incredibly dangerous criminal network which sadly included many corrupt members of society." These detectives are a credit to themselves and Scotland Yard.

The Deputy Chief nodded. His speech was finished. Jessica and Declan stood and received their applause. The Chief walked over to them and clipped a silver medal to their service blazer. He then walked over to the nearest camera and discussed the case. The whole thing was a giant fuck-you to everyone involved with the casino.

The Mayor approached the stand, coughing lightly to clear her throat.

"All the detectives on this city's fine police force deserve this and more for their services in bringing down the Blackened Hill Casino crime ring."

A flooding roar of applause swept across the crowd. Declan ran his hands through his hair in a calming way. Jessica walked off the stage and to her car. Ava was leaned against the passenger door. She gazed at Jessica. Jessica ran over and wrapped her arms around Ava's stomach. She ran her fingers down her shard shoulder blades and felt the line of her scar. Running her hands up to Ava's soft, warm neck as she pulled away. Ava stared at Jessica with love in her eyes, she leaned forward her tender lips pressing against Jessica's. The kiss contained such passion and desperation. The stain of Jessica's red lipstick smudged below Ava's lips. Jessica rubbed her thumb through the mark and removed it. She loved the feel of her lips.

Ava ran her hand down Jessica's arm and into Jessica's. She walked back and rested against the car. She playfully whispered, "Are you coming?"

She smiled at Jessica, her perfect teeth shining through her parted lips. She slightly bit her lip gently making the skin turn pink. She was so enticing, Jessica would have blindly followed her anywhere. She could feel her pulse rising inside her chest. She loosened her tie and threw her blazer onto the back seat.

They sat across from each other on the soft fabric sofa in Jessica's apartment. This time, Ava was entrapped in the beauty of Jessica. Her mouth fell open in lust as she spoke.

"Ava, you broke out of a police cell, you killed Francis Jaeger. I have to…"

Before she could finish her sentence, Ava kissed her again. Jessica laughed as the kiss deepened. Ava looked down at her and smiled. Jessica lay on Ava's knee and quickly fell asleep.

Ava ran her hand through Jessica's hair and watched her sleep. She rubbed the top of the scar on her back and stood up.

"I'm sorry, but no one can save me."

She pushed away the one person she knew could save her. She thought of the night they had spent together. Her eyes filled with sadness. She knew she could never allow herself to forget the screams as she was dragged through hell. She was the Fallen Angel and she had to stay alone.